THE JOY OF KILLING

THE JOY OF KILLING

a novel

HARRY N. MACLEAN

COUNTERPOINT
BERKELEY

Library of Congress Cataloging-in-Publication Data
MacLean, Harry N.
  The joy of killing : a novel / Harry MacLean.
     pages ; cm
1. Violence--Psychological aspects--Fiction. 2. Psychological fiction. I. Title.

PS3613.A27367J69 2015
813'.6--dc23

2015009478

ISBN 978-1-61902-742-8

Cover design by Kelly Winton
Interior Design by Megan Jones Design

COUNTERPOINT
2560 Ninth Street, Suite 318
Berkeley, CA 94710
www.counterpointpress.com

Printed in the United States of America

The joy of killing! the joy of seeing killing done—
these are traits of the human race at large.

—MARK TWAIN

For
Hulya O'Brien

THE GIRL

T HE STORY BEGINS in the middle of my fifteenth year on this earth. It was a mid-December evening in 1958, and I was returning home for Christmas from an eastern prep school, where I had been sent a year earlier in response to what a school psychologist referred to as "serious behavioral problems." I arrived in Grand Central Station on a train from the western hills of Massachusetts in the late morning. From there I would catch a train to Chicago, and from there another one to Des Moines, Iowa, where my parents would pick me up for the drive to Booneville.

In a fading light and cold wind, suitcase in hand, I tramped down the long walk to the last car and climbed the metal steps. I figured on settling in a window seat, lighting a weed, and checking out the sights as the train pulled out of the big city. Once rolling, I would walk up to the club car and see if I could talk the bartender into selling me a beer. I stopped at an empty row of seats and tossed my suitcase in the overhead rack. Across the aisle sat a girl, blonde, wearing a blue pleated skirt and dark sweater. Her face was turned away, but her bare legs lay sideways on the seat. The suitcase bumped down from the rack and knocked me on the shoulder. I thought I heard a muffled giggle from her direction. I jammed the suitcase back onto the rack, slipped out of my sports coat, loosened my tie, and sat down on the aisle seat.

The overhead lights threw a soft glare over the scene. People continued to climb aboard and bump their way down the aisle. I felt in my jacket pocket for the pack of Luckies I had bought at a newsstand in the station, along with a girlie magazine, and tore off the red stripe around the top edge. I extricated a weed from the pack and whacked it on the back of my Zippo. The train lurched forward, stopped; lurched again, stopped; then began creeping up the tracks, tilting suddenly to the left, and then to the right, like a wounded buffalo. I flipped open the Zippo with my thumb. I felt someone's eyes on me. I glanced across the aisle and saw the girl's face in the window. She brushed strands of hair from her face, while sliding her half-exposed legs from the seat and onto the floor. I snapped the Zippo shut.

She turned to face me. The corners of her pretty eyes were slightly downturned. Her lips were in a faint pout. Blonde hair tumbled to her shoulders. I tapped the cigarette on the lighter again. She spoke:

"Where are you going?"

I hesitated: I was not good with girls, particularly ones this pretty. She shifted slightly in her seat, revealing even more, whiter thigh. The conductor arrived, stopped between us.

"Tickets, please!"

I handed him mine. He stuck the stub in a clip on the overhead rack, his narrow blue-coated body blocking my view across the aisle. "Chicago," he said, and placed a stub in the clip above the girl, and then moved on. Her skirt was now tucked under her legs. The clickety-clack of the wheels grew louder.

"Chicago. I mean Des Moines. And then Booneville."

"I can barely hear you," she said. "Why don't you come over and sit with me? It's a long trip." She patted the seat next to her.

I stuffed the Luckies in my shirt pocket and lay the weed and Zippo on top of the girlie magazine on the inside seat. I rose and stepped into the aisle. She removed her hand and seemed to guide me into the seat with her eyes. I sat slightly turned, as she was, and struggled to keep my eyes from dropping to her thighs, which seemed even whiter up close. Before I could say anything, she spoke.

"You're a preppie, aren't you?"

"Yeah."

"I go to a girls' school in Connecticut."

I held out my hand to introduce myself. She touched my arm lightly before I could speak.

"All those dark cold months without anyone to hold you, or make out with."

"We had dances with girls' schools," I said.

"God, they were terrible," she said. "I went to one dance. My date was the fullback on the St. Mark's football team. I never went again."

"You're pretty," I said. "I'm sure the boys wanted to dance with you."

She smiled. Her eyes held onto mine.

"It's going to be a long night," she said as she brushed back a blonde lock. She tilted her chin up a little. "Would you like to kiss me?"

I was stunned. After a moment, her eyes fluttered closed and her chin tilted up a little more. I leaned forward awkwardly. Her hand tucked under my chin and brought me in slowly, almost furtively, until our lips touched. Her tongue pressed between my teeth. I kissed her back, and she opened her mouth wider. She lay her hand on mine, lifted it slowly in the air, into the small space between us. I wanted to open my eyes, but before the clouds in my mind could clear my hand came to rest lightly on her breast, like a bird on a bush.

SITTING HERE, NOW, some forty years later, at the wooden table, tapping out these words on the Underwood in the soft light of a tall gooseneck lamp, not immune to the starlit sky out the window, nor the sounds and shadows of the rustling branches on the tall oak, I accept that the way I tell the story of that night on the train might not be the way it actually happened, in specific detail, in exact rhythm and tone and sequence; this version has received a little lacquer here and there as life piled up on it; to simplify it or make it feel better or cleaner, a few facts have possibly been dropped out or slipped in; perhaps even a few images have been recolored or restored to a brightness they never had. That's what time and the mind do, for better or worse, and only a fool would deny it. Through the window I can see the purple black between the stars, and the moon rising in the corner, and I think this night, as that one, can't last; the black will begin to fade slowly to gray, and the morning light will bring with it the end.

Perhaps it would be best to leave the story alone, to let the reel run in my head, unshared, until the very last frame, by which time I would probably appreciate it more, with time growing short, and some considerable ground left to cover, although I've already begun editing much of it out in my head. As the night has grown darker and the stars brighter I've considered letting go of these final pages altogether, drifting through it all, without direction, letting the past overflow the present until it is the present; there will be no sensation of coming loss, because everything has already happened, and the first glimmer of light in the distant sky beyond the walls will be like a moment of grace, into which I can move once and for all, perhaps into a final moment of undisturbed harmony.

I trust that the feelings of despair from unknowing will soon be gone, to be replaced by unwavering clarity, which may indeed bring its own form of despair, welcome only because of the absence of confusion, which is all I've ever asked for.

MY BREATH CAUGHT. At home, if you went steady with a girl, you might be able to feel her up, and after several months you might get inside her blouse, and if you hung in long enough to be "serious" you might get to feel her bare flesh, but it was a long and arduous process. It was certainly never the girl's idea. It occurred to me that I might be dreaming. Or that it might be some sort of a setup.

Her tongue darted around in my mouth like a butterfly, and my fingers responded by squeezing her breast. She turned slightly in the seat, to face me. I shifted to release my right hand, which was caught between my hip and the seat. It rose in the air and settled lightly on her left breast. Both hands now pressed in. A soft sound rose from the girl's throat, which I took as encouragement. When my fingers found a nub of flesh, I tugged on it gently, and it stiffened. My dick bent hard against my zipper. I gave both nipples a twist and felt a tremble in her body.

A child screamed from somewhere in the back of the car. A loud crack and a whoosh of air blew in from the front. I saw a shadow moving slowly up the aisle. The conductor. Coming this way. The door hissed and shut and the loud clicking-clacking faded. The form stopped beside us, the round hat with a gold badge blocking a circle of dim light. I could see through his wireless spectacles professional, unfriendly eyes, which came to rest on me. A scrawny finger pushed the spectacles up his nose. I waited for him to say something, but instead his eyes shifted away and up to the rack across the aisle, over my seat. He reached up and flicked my stub from the clip and turned and placed it in the clip over us, next to the girl's. He moved on, rolling with the sway of the train, like a sailor on a ship.

The light in the car now seemed a murky yellow, except for a sharp reading light on at the very front, and the only sound was a soft snoring somewhere behind us.

"I guess you're stuck here, with me," the girl said.

MY HANDS RISE from the typewriter and settle onto my lap. I look at the scene more closely, at the man standing in the aisle, the conductor, and I notice his gold watch chain traversing his blue vest, from west to east, like a river of gold, and I think perhaps I've added it in, this small glitter. Was it really there? It doesn't matter, and I've long since lost the ability to sort out those things, what is true or not, or what is real or not. If something happened or not. I've painted in the gold chain on the blue expanse, and there it will be, there it will stay, and if I were to view the scene again, it will appear as always having been there. Sitting here now, I believe that to be the truth. Simply because things become more apparent over time doesn't mean they weren't always there. You just didn't see them. Perhaps I've added the spectacles along the line, and the ticket punch in his hand. But not the girl. Not the girl. She lived that night with me on the train, and she loved me, for those few hours at least, and she has provided me with great sustenance and solace over the years. To see her now, to hold her face in my hands, feel the heat, to march through the garden and into the water with her in my heart would be my final desire, and why I am writing now, to etch her into my brain so that even faltering steps or timorous fear can't erase her. If anyone examined my brain, they would think as they watched the scene, what a lucky boy he is, the way he just stumbled into this play, and, really, he handled it fairly well, for the little that he knew, and he must have gone on to great things, with women and otherwise, so smooth he seemed, and they would be amused at the scene with the conductor, and find themselves erotically pulsed by the drama.

In some ways, I prefer that boy to the man sitting here at the wooden desk, in the small room at the very top of the stairs, looking out into the sky and the dark clouds sailing over the water, pondering and preparing, which is why I bring him back, bring them both back, for times like this. It's how I've stayed reasonably sane over the years; for I am able sometimes to freeze a single frame of that journey in my consciousness, and let it be all there is.

I work on the narrative of that night, clicking and clacking, picking and pecking, watching the words float on and off the page, remaining sufficiently present to finish the story. To achieve some elusive sense of completion, and, as well, something to stand as my last will and testament.

THE DOOR AT the front of the car closed behind the conductor. The light seemed to dim. I turned to the girl with some apprehension, but she was smiling seductively at me. As soon as all was still, her hand tugged gently on the bottom of her sweater. Then her fingers disappeared. Paused, twisted, rose, paused, twisted. She was undo- ing the buttons on her blouse. Her tongue caressed her top lip, as if to make absolutely clear to me what was happening, and her eyes radiated like lures for the hare on the edge of the forest. Unsure of what to do or say, I could only watch. Her hand reappeared and rested on her lap. She tilted her head, and I leaned in to kiss her, and this time she was quite gentle. She opened her eyes, slightly glazed, and in an easy, whispery voice I would remember the rest of my days said, "They're yours."

I felt a little strange, perhaps because it was me she was offer- ing her breasts to, or perhaps it was her boldness. I glanced about the car, then looked closely at the protrusions of her dark sweater. Hesitate any longer and she might change her mind, I told myself. My left hand rose and nudged its way under the sweater. One fin- ger and then two slipped under the edge of the blouse, touched the unseen flesh, brushed over her ribs. The fingers spread open a fraction and began slipping upward, until the tips reached the place where the thin flesh over the bones turned to substance, strangely firm and spongy. No bra. My hand trembled. Her fingers touched my cheek. My thumb slid around until her breast was caught in the semicircle of my thumb and forefinger. I squeezed ever so slightly and felt the mound rise. My heart clenched—this was happening, the girl, her breast, my hand, and God only knew where it was lead- ing, although I knew where I hoped it would. *The nipple.* My hand moved up a little further until the second and third fingers were also touching it. Finally I believed her: I could do with them as I pleased. A flush of blood hit my groin.

I caught the sweaty perfume, and I kissed her neck and tasted a flowery bitterness. My thumb pressed down on the nipple, and it disappeared in the mound, only to spring back, harder, like a pencil eraser. Her back arched slightly, and the nipple bumped into my thumb. I pinched it gently, and she pushed up a little more. I gave it a twist, and she murmured something in my ear. I felt her other hand on my neck, pulling me in closer, and sensed the desperation in her. She whispered again: "Please." My dick pushed so hard into my zipper it hurt. My hand spread wide, thumb moving across the space to touch the other nipple, my little finger still pressing into the first one. I tugged them both gently. Her lips were against my ear. I felt the heat of her whisper.

"Harder."

Damn. I always thought nipples were delicate. I twisted one, then the other. I pinched the very tip of it, and, hearing, feeling nothing, pinched it even harder. Her chest shook, and I heard the same word again, so I pressed in harder until my nails met each other through the flesh. Her body froze in position, her breath released, and strange, foreign sounds came from her. A shiver went through her body. A low moan brushed my ear.

I ROCK MY chair back, close my eyes, and think that with the clarity and finite complexity of the images that come into my mind, unbidden or otherwise, I should have been a painter, because there was little else I could do with them; the images came and went as

they pleased, often to my delight or amusement, but often otherwise, to my distraction or distress. There was the time in my early
thirties when I met Shelley Duvall at a reception for the film festival
in Des Moines. As we were talking, I became quite taken with her
long, white neck, graceful as a swan's, and suddenly from ear to
ear a thin red line edged across the middle of it, half an inch above
the clavicle, as if someone had just flicked the tip of a straight razor
through the flesh. She kept on talking, unaware of the cut, so pre-
cise was it, until tiny red drops appeared just below the line, and
her head began to wobble a little, and still she kept on smiling and
chatting. I could not bear to watch her head tilt like that, fearing
it would eventually topple off, and as the red drops began to slide
down the slender neck I disengaged—her hand was resting lightly
on my forearm, and had been for at least a minute, which in these
sorts of things is a long time—mumbling something lame and turning to walk away, leaving her hand still poised in the air where my
forearm had been, a smile freezing on her slightly surprised face.

I haven't seen that image in awhile. As sharp and bright as the
day it was born, if not sharper, and almost as frightening, in its
red and white, Valentine's Day cleaved beauty. I feel a twinge of
annoyance. The image of Shelley in red skews me off track and
reminds me of how little influence I have over the stuff in my
head, and how I have often felt the intrusions only as a burden,
only recently beginning to see it—this story, the one of the girl on
the train—as a path to freedom. I glance at the keys on the typewriter, and then at my fingers, as if willing them to rise and tap
out something perceptive or perhaps enlightening. I hear strange

sounds from the floor below, like a toy rattle being shaken back and forth. And then it stops. This morning I searched every room in the four-story house—it's an old place with lots of out-of-the-way crooks and nooks—and as darkness grew close I bolted the doors one by one and ascended the flights to the small room at the top, with a window overlooking the lovely garden and the high stone wall and the lake beyond. The moon, I notice, seems stuck in the lower right corner of the window. I lean a little to my left and see that it's caught between two limbs in the tall oak, whose great branches arch out like veins in the sky. Images, you see, can mutate with time or remain as crystal clear as the instant they were born. Shelley doesn't particularly bother me, mainly because she's fixed and her head no longer wobbles, but there are thousands of others, if not thousands of thousands, some seen some not seen, that arrive and depart as they please, and you can either adjust and weave them into whatever else is going on in your reality or disengage yourself from them—no easy task, I assure you—or if you can do neither, pray that they dissipate in some harmless way that doesn't leave you stranded. Many of them, it seems, involve either sex or violence, or sex and violence. I should say that the night of the reception I ended up having sex with Shelley. I came just as the thin red line across her neck split open. The image of the girl on the train is, as I said, really a hundred thousand images, or more, and sometimes I can stop the progression where I please, and start it again with the flick of an eyelash, and each time there is something new, a taste, a look; the light in the train might be more yellow-diffused than in the past, or it dims occasionally as the train

rocks from the edge of one wheel to the edge of the other. The passing lights of the farmhouses and crossings and occasional highway
cars streak together into a blur against the black outside. I doubt I
saw much of anything that night, so consumed was I by my other
senses: the creaking footfalls of the conductor as he makes his way
up and down the aisle, the smell of garlic from the dinner basket
of an elderly couple up ahead, the insistent rhythm of the clacking
of the wheels, and the stale, cigarette-stained air that ripples when
someone opens one of the doors, (when the clacking is so loud you
don't notice the fresh air until the door crashes shut) and the varied
smells of human beings in some sort of repose after their efforts at
living another day have come to an end.

I SOUGHT TO remove my hand from beneath the sweater gently,
but the girl pressed it against her breast. I wanted to tell her how
amazing it was I had finally met her, how much I loved her for it,
she was so much more beautiful than I had ever imagined, and her
skin was so smooth, under my fingertips. She put a finger to my lips.

Suddenly, lights were flashing by in the window, white lights
on top of warehouses, lights encircling silos, and flashing red lights
on white cross arms, and yellow lights in house windows, and the
train whistled three loud blasts, and I thought that nothing of this
night could survive the sort of glare that crossing into the outskirts
of a Midwestern farm town like Toledo would bring, an unfriendly,
grim bleakness that would bust up anyone's dream, ruin the sounds
and smells of it, and I was thinking of what I might say to ease the
transition when there was one long, loud blast of the whistle and

the rocket darkened, shook from side to side, and shot forward. I wondered what happens now; maybe we cuddle like this for the rest of the trip, and maybe—although, seriously, I doubted it—maybe I could at some fortunate moment slip a hand *below the waist*—a place unknown to me, and truthfully a place I found a little scary to even imagine. At no time yet in my life had I even come close to it, and even in my fantasies I seldom got that far—an image of a girl, like the one in my arms, standing in front of a mirror in pink panties, where you could just make out the crease in her bottom, was a favorite and far more than sufficient. As if sensing this, the girl raised her face to mine, allowing her eyes to darken even deeper, saying in better form than words that this story was far from over.

My finger caught the edge of the lower lip and pulled it down a little, and in the dimness I could see a little indentation in the middle. I leaned into kiss her, and I could feel the spot with my tongue. She caught my finger in her lips and sucked gently. I felt her tongue circle my finger. My throat constricted. Her hand tugged at my belt buckle, and the prong easily sprung free from the leather. I thought of touching her hand, guiding it away. I was embarrassed, for myself, over the bulge in my pants. Her fingers wrested open the top button on the slacks and then tugged the zipper down. The flaps spread open. Her hand slid down and then back up my dick. She tightened her grip, and it occurred to me that what was happening might be just a hand job—just a hand job!—and I felt my throat relax a little. Still something to brag about back at school, if I wanted to. Slowly she lowered her head onto me, and I felt her tongue probe around the perimeter, as if looking for something. I twitched, and she dropped all the way down. The blood rushed in my ears. I lay a hand on her head. I felt the tip of my dick brush the back of her throat and her lips pull at the very base of it. Too much, I thought. I'm a goner. I let my fingers sink into the hair. If I intended a signal, she missed it, for now she lifted all the way up until her lips were barely touching me, pausing long enough for the cool air to brush the skin, and then descended slowly, a millimeter at a time.

OVER THE YEARS I've often wondered whether it was simply the particular circumstances of the evening, the lonely metal capsule rocking back and forth as it plowed through the darkness, the proximity of unseen strangers, the faintly flickering stars, that brought the two of us together. There are times when you go beyond words, beyond even images, or sensations, and then you come to see that the process of recovering those times will inevitably fail, and fail so severely that it will make you wonder whether there's any point in trying to describe it. You know that something dear will be lost by the doing of it; some inner life of the time will be flattened out, and it will become a good deal less precious than before. Sitting in front of the typewriter, banging on these keys, I feel a slight disloyalty to the girl, that I am ruining something that should have remained unwritten, forever. Maybe the night on the train meant nothing to her. She probably forgot about it the minute she stepped off the train in Chicago, already thinking about seeing her boyfriend that night. A real heart breaker, other boys would say. Living her life as she saw fit, leaving a trail of wreckage in her wake. I never felt that about her, over the years. The only harm I suffered was the establishment of hope—that one day I would find her, or someone like her, again. Because it was a perfect experience, and you can chase one of those for all your days, measuring all else against it, and come up exhaustingly short. Now and then, I've wondered if it really happened; if she really existed, or if I read it somewhere, or heard it from another boy, or if maybe some of it happened, and I've embellished it greatly, but I swear to God, I can feel the train car sway back and forth; I can see her throat white in the stars' pale light, feel her hair brush my cheek, lost in it, the perfect alignment, not a molecule out of place, giving way, marred only by a tiny voice of warning.

Yes, sometimes I can freeze the image almost anywhere in the scene—her eyes, pleased, even slightly amused, holding a bit of a challenge in them, glancing up at me—and for almost as long as I want, in color or black and white, with or without sound, or I can roll it a frame every few seconds or so, and fall back into the night and absorb it all over again, into my very being.

She had to know it was my first time; thank God she was kind about it. I let my hand slide slowly down her back, on top of the sweater, feeling the ridges of her spine, slowly, lower and lower, until I felt the band of her skirt. I thought, man, she doesn't even know your name, nor you hers, and I got it then, that this was the whole point, separation of body and soul. My fingers crept under the edge of her skirt and touched actual skin, and she stopped moving, as if to see how far I was going to go, and I decided not much further. Suddenly, the train rocked to the right hard enough to cause

fingertips to slide down another fraction, where they unintention-
ally touched the very top of the crevice, and my first thought was,
Jesus Christ, she's not wearing any panties! The velvet feel of the
soft rise of her bottom was too much, and I pulled my fingers back.

I worried that I had gone too far, but I felt her fingers creep up
my chest and begin unbuttoning my shirt, first the middle button,
then one button on either side of it. She glanced up at me, and in
those strangely beautiful eyes there was now a touch of merriment.
She laid her head on my chest, and her fingers slid under the edge
of the shirt and pinched my right nipple. It hurt. I laid my hand on
her head and pulled gently on a lock of hair to discourage her. She
closed her teeth on me. I sucked in a breath, whispered, "Fuck."
Now she clamped her teeth on the very bottom, and shook her
head slightly, and the annoyance turned into little shivers of pain. I
pulled back, which only hurt more. She saw the look of discomfort
on my face and looked pleased with herself. I got it then; realizing that the end was near for me, she had distracted me from my
course, and she had done it quite well, for my dick, which she still
held lightly in one hand, was now half its former self, and both it
and I were a good deal less excited than a few moments earlier.

THE SOUND OF the doorbell chiming its brash two-note tune
always manages to penetrate the thickest blankets of consciousness,
usually in simple moments, like when I'm packing my briefcase in
the morning, or lacing up a boot. On that hot summer day, the
metallic sounds stirred up in me a terrible dread. I watched as my
mother walked by the living room to the front door, and I jumped

in my chair when it rang again. I remember the patches of light patterned on the floor from the bright sun streaming through the blinds in the front window; the purple iris pattern on the arms of the chair in which I was sitting; and the polished silver cigarette box on the glass coffee table next to a *Life* magazine. I can even see the scuffed toes of my black cowboy boots on the beige carpet. I can't imagine why I was sitting there on a midsummer morning; I should have been out on my green-and-white Schwinn, making the rounds of my hangouts. The sounds of the front door opening, a short pause, and my mother's voice:

"Yes?"

I leaned over to look down the hall to the doorway, where she was standing, one hand on the doorknob and the other on her hip. All I can make out through her limbs is a gray hat, a fedora. Perhaps I saw more then; but that's the image that's survived. One gray hat with a dark band around the crown and a brim tipped down slightly in front.

"Mrs. Jackson?"

It was the voice of doom. I knew that from the sturdy, cold tone. It told her what was coming was going to be tough, steel yourself, I am going to totally fuck up your morning, as well as your son's, the boy at the center of all this. It's my job, and it's part of life. Nothing personal.

"Yes."

She got it, too. This wasn't about previous incidents with the school principals or department store security. This was dead serious grown-up stuff.

These images, the doorbell, the hat, particularly the hat—for it was bright that morning and in the background now I can see trees and perhaps even a house—emerge in pieces, or together in some incoherent fashion, or hooked to whatever else fits their fancy; they flash like a camera bulb or they seep up from the depth; a semblance of coherence might begin to emerge, if you will it to, at your own risk, and you think year after year you've glued one shard properly onto another and if you live long enough the whole story will reveal itself. I trust nothing, though. Whatever the latest version, it's only that: the latest version, stimulated and melded and twisted by all else that's roiling in the great miasma. The very mind that is fucked up is trying to make up the story of why it's fucked up. You can see the source of the despair; there is nothing unchanging, immutable, which would be fine if the story was successfully blown out of consciousness, or jammed so deep that none of it ever oozed to the surface, and thus the effects of it were never traceable; you knew only that somewhere something lay beyond your ken, and you left whatever it was alone, and lived as best you could.

MY FINGERTIPS ARE beginning to hurt from banging on the stiff keys. I would like to sit back in my chair and close my eyes, but I dare not; the moment the faintest light creases the darkness, the time for this will have passed, and the matter will be done. I will be done. My eyes are drawn to the table. The wood is lightly stained rough oak. It shows cuts and pocks, scars of use. I wonder about people who have sat here in front of it over the years. A young woman in a cotton print dress reading a telegraph from the Department of War telling of the death of her husband on an island in the middle of the Pacific. She whispers the words and weeps into her hands. She sees images of him dying on the beach, torn flesh caught on twisted metal in the watery sand. Time goes by, and eventually she remarries and has kids. She serves her new family meals at this very table, but the images of death on that island continue to flitter in and out of the story of her life, vivid but unstable. Her husband's shattered body turning sideways in the sand as the tide comes in is the image in her mind in the final moments of her life.

I went through the table drawer several hours ago and found a few sheets of linen paper with a name and the address of the place imprinted on them in an elaborate dark blue scroll. I see a man in an expensively tailored summer suit sitting at the table and writing a letter to acquaintances in Italy. He is arranging their visit the following summer and is inquiring of the woman's preference in vintage wine. Her husband was his roommate at Oxford University many years ago, and he is haunted by images of a homosexual encounter between them one drunken evening in their flat at the end of the school year. The man's mouth on his cock, a lock of hair falling over his eye. Waking in the cold light to their still entangled limbs. He seduced the man's wife when he visited them in Rome three years back, in order, he thinks now, to push aside those images, but unfortunately they all tend to run together into one tawdry erotic jumble, particularly when he's been drinking heavily, which he has been tonight. He thinks that perhaps during the couple's stay he should bring the three of them together in bed.

He throws back his tumbler of scotch, his mind already conjuring up the sights, the feels, the smells of the scene. He considers for a moment suggesting it in the letter, but thinks better of it. They will all need to be drinking, and at the right moment he will simply ask if he can watch the two of them make love, and then, when they're in the heat of it, he'll find away to join in. The man pours another tumbler and bends in to finish the letter. It must appear to be spontaneous, he decides. Or better, the woman's idea.

A LOUD SCREECHING of metal on metal—you can picture the sparks flying—was followed by two cries of the train whistle. The train jerked, and the girl's fingers tightened on my nipples. I flinched, and she giggled, and the brakes sounded again like wild-flying banshees. The train slowed. The sounds of other people stirring; the baby resumed crying. The snoring stopped. A nasal voice complained. The girl leaned in, gave each one of my nipples a tender kiss, and began buttoning up my shirt. The train lurched to a stop. We sat there. I looked out the window—we were nowhere; no lights, no highways, no buildings. Not even trees. Lit only vaguely by a dying moon off to the east and a few scattered stars. I pictured masked men on horses galloping up to the train with six-guns flashing in their hands.

"Something ahead on the track," a male voice called out from the front of the car. That confirmed it. We're being robbed, by a gang of train bandits.

"It's a holdup," I said to the girl.

"You're funny," she said.

"I'm serious," I said, leaning over her for a better look outside. A shadow moved away rapidly in the pale light. "It's the Brandon-Younger gang," I whispered.

Now she looked at me curiously, saw that I was serious, and became serious herself. "What's happening?" she asked.

"Just pretend you're asleep. They're after the payroll in the mail car. If we're lucky, they won't have time to rob us."

I could hear the whinny and stomping of horses, the barking of orders, the clanging of heavy doors being thrown open, some vain protests, a thunk and a cry as a pistol butt cracked a skull. I pulled the girl's coat up to her shoulders.

All we had to do now was not get shot up during the robbery. Another day I would have confronted them—I had run a cowboy gang myself, in my earlier years—but now I had the girl to worry about, and the rest of the trip, although it was beginning to seem as if events were conspiring against us. Loud voices outside a car or two up ahead, arguing, a loud shout followed by two shots. A double cross, I thought. When you had something valuable, someone else always wanted it. I felt the girl stiffen. "Easy," I said. "It'll be over soon." There would either be a shootout, or whoever got the money would hightail it across the barren plains with the others in hot pursuit. The passengers would be forgotten, and in a few minutes the train would limp on without its treasure. More shouts, and shots, and then a raucous pounding of hooves, shadows ripping across the flatland in the slimmest light of the moon. I felt a shot of envy over the outlaws' freedom to rove and fly about in the wind, and to die a dramatic death if God so willed it. I could have been a Ghost Rider in the Sky, trailing steers breathing fire across the endless expanse, and maybe I still could. I felt a hand on my cheek. The girl's face was tilted up to me now, and I saw concern in her beautiful eyes.

I squeezed her shoulders, as if to say it's all right. I realized the trade-off; you could ride across the endless sky forever or you could have the girl. Not both. I had chosen the girl, and I was glad I had. The robbers would be reaching their canyon hideout about now, and those left would be dividing up the spoils, which could never match up to the gift of this girl's gratitude. I kissed her firmly, and with barely a thought I slipped a hand under her sweater and captured a breast. The train jerked and inched forward.

I HEAR THE strange rattling sound again. The wind somewhere, I think, but the branches on the oak are still now, although I notice that the moon seems to have dislodged itself from the limbs and is creeping up the sky like a loosened clot. It sounds again, near the back of the house, probably in the kitchen, four stories down. A raccoon has gotten in. I've seen them in the garden; they are not scared of me. But it's a *rattling* sound, not a knocking, or a banging. Something metal inside a tin box, like large paper clips, or nails, with an odd rhythm to it. Then it stops. Now the night is soundless. I hold perfectly still until I can feel the blood pounding in my ear. I give the roller on the typewriter a hard twist backward, to read a line or two of what I've written. The dark hat band, the light in the trees in the background, my mother's print dress in the door light, would float away for long periods, then come tumbling back in. I knew the path the images would lead me down if I paid enough attention to them, and I did sometimes, in bursts of courage, for I had never forgotten the crux of what happened that day, or rather another earlier day, although as I grew older and learned the fickleness of memory I would look for clues that I had patched the story together from here and there. I never spoke of it to anyone, and it was only in recent years that I began to wonder about the formative effects of it, particularly in things that had played out badly in my life. I was then barely twelve years old. And the whole thing hadn't been my idea. Yes, I went along with it, but only because of the promises that were made. It was stupid to believe them. How little we see of what makes us who we are, of what pushes us this way rather than that. Fortunate are those who don't give a fuck, but if you do there's nothing you can do about it except drink or do drugs or piss off the peak of the highest mountain. Or sit down at a desk on a night with a moon rising over the waters and write the ending of the story.

The rattling again, fainter this time, as if whatever it is has retreated to some corner in the cellar.

So the boy in the train is just a boy and does not know what ails him, for in his mind at that moment nothing ails him. What is happening he hasn't even dreamed of, and he doesn't know to worry that it might never happen again or about how it's going to feel when the train ride is over.

I CLOSED MY eyes as her head descended again. I understood that I would go off when she decided, and not a moment sooner or later, and that was OK. I wondered if I might be able to count this as my second blow job, inasmuch as my dick had gone almost completely soft during the holdup. I had no idea what was in her mind right now; she could be comparing my dick to the size of her boyfriend's. The girl paused, as if hearing my thoughts. This time she left her hand at the base of it and went down until her mouth bumped into her fingers. I was suddenly overcome not just by what was happening but *the idea* of what was happening. The hardest to fathom was the girl; she was enchanting, with soft lips and lovely, uncertain eyes. That was why she chose me tonight; she saw something not quite right.

I'm caught in the image of the blonde hair splayed on my lap, rising and falling to some unheard rhythm, when another image, startling in its clarity, intrudes into the story. There it is, shining like a black pearl in white sand: my first wife on her hands and knees on the bedroom floor, with my best friend poised behind her. He is inserting his cock slowly, carefully into her. One hand reaches around for a handful of hair, and the other palm pushes down squarely on her ass. She backs into his cock and winces. After four or five thrusts, he reaches around and grabs her tits. He begins fucking against his hands. Her face is frozen in a noiseless cry, and he can see it because he has her facing the mirror on the closet door.

The three of us had come back drunk from a party, and I'd made us another round of drinks. Half an hour went by, and my wife said she was wiped out and going to bed. After a few minutes, my friend went to the kitchen to get more drinks. Minutes passed, and more minutes, and I didn't hear anything. Finally some dim

alert sounded in my brain, and I rose and glanced in the kitchen—
no friend, no drinks. I heard sounds coming from down the hall,
like some sort of assault. I proceeded down the hall, until I came to
the bedroom door. It was half open. I pushed it a few inches more.
When I saw him poised over her like that, I could also see the rub-
bery outlines of her pussy, and I figured from the look of it and
the position they were in that he must have started fucking her the
moment he walked in.

That image is one that never mutates or blurs or bleeds or decol-
orizes. Vivid and sharp, willing to materialize at the best or worst
of times. He pulled his cock out so just the tip of the head remained
inside. My wife shook her ass, and he pushed in knowingly, as if
he had been fucking her for years, and I wondered if perhaps he
had been fucking her for years. He caught me looking at them in
the mirror, grabbed her ass and squeezed hard as if to confirm that
it belonged to him now. These images live on in a world of their
own, appearing without regard to what I'm doing or thinking or
what else might be in my head at the moment or the consequences
thereof. There is never anything I can do about it, except, as in
this case, try to limit the intrusion to one image, or two, rather
than running the whole tape through to the very end where she
is crying and begging him to come and finally his body clenches
and he bellows like a wounded bull. Just like the image of the gray
fedora and the fleshy creased face below it could seep into the most
innocuous moment and leave in me the realization that most likely
the sights and sounds of that scene would accompany me to the
grave. I sometimes saw it as a form of insanity, the unwelcome

intrusion of another reality into my own; although on occasion I would let the sights spin on their own way so it would be me behind my wife, slamming in and jarring her head down onto my friend's cock. The details and vividness of it felt as real as anything else in my life. I had learned some resistance to the images of the men at the door—they both wore sport coats, slacks and ties, cheap Sears stuff, except for the fedoras—but it always gave way in the end, and more pieces hooked together, and the colors grew shaper, and the voices more distinct, and the look on my mother's face more disgusted. I can feel it in my gut, as I sit here writing. And you can see another serious problem with this porousness: it flavors and affects everything else I'm doing or thinking about. Like now—the image of my wife and friend is severely interfering with my recollection of that night on the train and my ability to relive it here on paper, which is troubling, because over the years the train ride has come to mean a good deal more to me than my first wife, and, although you can never be sure, I think it's been immune to the ravages of time and experience. The girl's lovely face is as smooth and flawless as Chinese porcelain. There's little to do about the intrusion, except to let it run its course and try to hold onto some slender thread of consciousness in the meantime.

I PUSH MY chair back and stand. I feel a draft rising from under the door and listen closely for the rattling sounds. I walk around the desk to the window, hoping that this slight change of atmosphere will allow space for the girl on the train to reemerge and for us to continue our drama unalloyed. The oval-shaped window, framed in wood, grows larger as I approach. Through it I see the moon, now lit with fire, has reached the middle of the sky, halfway between the top of the world and the icy waters below. The branches of the tall oak are motionless. I remember the follies of the wind here: from a dead stillness to a raging gale in a couple of breaths. The garden wall, constructed over a century ago of lake rock, casts a shadow over the garden. Just beyond the wall, out of view, is a cliff, and thirty yards below that lays a necklace of sharp rocks barely submerged in the black water. The lake itself is so large there is no distant shoreline. In summer storms, sailing boats overturned and people drowned. Our parents rented this house every August for all the summers of my youth. In my old room, one floor below where I'm standing, I'd found the gooseneck lamp on the same table where it had always been. My chair by the window where I used to sit and watch the moon rise was gone.

Our father always reminded us first thing on arriving here that we were never to climb the wall or play on the cliff or on the rocks below it. So we took our lunch sacks and fishing poles and walked a quarter mile down the dirt road to a bay, where a river ran into the lake and formed a small beach.

Back then, the door to this room, at the bottom of the stairs, was always locked, as was the door to the cellar. We never knew where the people who lived here went in the summer, or what they thought of us, the family who took over their house every August and sat at their table and slept in their beds and used their toilets. The house has been vacant and unused for years, I overheard today at the little grocery in town. Too run down, too costly to fix up

now. I found my way to the place just as daylight was beginning
to fade, after visiting the bay down the road, where I saw that the
rope we rode out over the river had been taken down, although
you could still see the groove carved in the sturdy tree limb arched
over the water. The north woods lake water was cold as ice, even in
August, although it didn't seem to bother us, or if it did we didn't
let it show. First one in. Last one out. The trick on the rope swing
was to let go at the very peak, so you flew as far and high as possible, but still managed to land short of the submerged branches on
the opposite bank. I zero in on the face of the boy as he approaches
the rope swing for a flicker of knowing. I see nothing. From the
looks of him, approaching six feet, butch cut, ribs sticking out,
gold ring with a glass ruby on his right hand, this is about a year
before the girl on the train, and a couple years after the detectives.
And yet not a glimmer, not here, in the warm summer sun. Hour
after hour we played, until our father came to fetch us home. It was
moments like this, when you look back closely and don't see con-
firming details, that you began to doubt the whole story and think
maybe it was another conglomeration that your mind had served
up and you had come to accept through time and repetition. But
not the fedoras, or the girl on the train; I would swear to death by
either one. I could hear right now the dull thrumming of the detective's voice as he spoke to my mother. The second detective was
younger, with a thin mustache and motionless eyes. He took off his
dark brown fedora and held it in one hand as my mother stepped
back and opened the door for them. The way it plays now, the first
man, with the glasses and fleshy face, pulls a wallet from his coat

pocket and opens it to show a gold badge, although that might be one of the images that has bled in over time. The girl on the train happened because I can remember the smallest detail of it, such as the raw look of her mouth when she finally lifted her head from my lap, although as I've said, I don't doubt a few details might have dropped in; perhaps the ticket punch in the conductor's hand, or the baby crying.

I would stand on the bank in the sun, dripping wet, and feel the warmth of the summer wind slowly drying the drops on my skin, and you might think that in an unprotected moment like that something from the past might slip through. Maybe it was the power of the adolescent mind to believe that once you get the rock out of your shoe the pain was over. Maybe I was so happy in those days at the lake that the past simply didn't exist. After lights-out, I would bend the gooseneck lamp down low to the bedside table and in the glow of it masturbate to a girl in one of the magazines I'd brought from home. Unimpeded in the slightest by images of whatever had gone before. This place, the bay, the house, the pathways along the lakeshore, with its evening-long lingering sunsets, had seemed separate and safe from the outside world of remembrance.

It's early autumn now, a time we were never here. The days are shorter, and the evening winds are sharper, and the moon sits higher in the sky. The edges of the oak leaves are just beginning to turn. A boy drowned in the lake one summer. His family lived a couple of houses down, closer to the bay where we swam. The canoe tipped over a ways out and the boy disappeared. I can see his face now—straw-colored hair, freckles—and even remember his name. Joseph. Not Joe. Joseph. From the porch we watched the boats dragging the lake; we were sent to bed when it was still light, and I could hear the motors chugging as I drifted off. The next morning I was scared to go to the lake for fear of seeing Joseph in the water, but he was found washed up in a woody tangle half a mile down from our little bay. Blue and with his eyes stuck open, we'd heard. I'd almost forgotten the incident until early this evening, when the caretaker and I were standing on the porch in the failing light. He was holding the large set of house keys, flicking one after another on the brass ring, and at one point his eyes locked on me. I remembered Joseph then. The caretaker was his father.

I STEP BACK, allowing the oval window to again frame the night scene. The moon has split the lake with a bright golden stripe. I sort through, as I have for the past several weeks, the threads of cloth to find the one connecting to the gray fedora. The first time the hat appeared, I think, was, during the wedding ceremony for my first marriage. A woman standing to the side of the altar was singing "Amazing Grace," and one of the notes must have sounded like our old doorbell, because suddenly the door opened and there the detective stood, in his hat and ill-fitting sports jacket, solemn eyes appraising the situation. The scene rolled on for a few frames—my mother backed up a step and turned and called over her shoulder to my father, who was in the den—until I sensed the looks of both the minister and the bride. My friend, the guy who would fuck the bride a few years later, held out the ring for me to take and slip on her finger. Everyone was smiling, so I smiled, too, in spite of the fading image in my head, which I finally managed to obscure by focusing on the small projections on the front of the bride's wedding dress.

"COME BACK," I murmur. I sit back down at the typewriter and settle my fingers on the keyboard. The girl slowly raised her head up until my dick popped out of her mouth; and—I mean this literally—I felt an intense pain as the cool air rushed the head. Her lips pressed into mine. I reached my right hand under her sweater and ran it up the flesh until I came to the soft mound.

She sat up and slowly lifted her sweater over her breasts. I glanced around, then back: even in the diffusion I could see that the breasts were perfectly symmetrical and several shades lighter than the rest of her. The nipples were more button-like than I had imagined, a little darker, as was the surrounding area. "Jesus," I whispered. She pulled the sweater up a little further, and my hands rose slowly and reached for them, fingers spreading as if to pluck fruit from a tree. I gently bunched each breast between my thumb and fingers until the nipples protruded out like dark cannon on a hilltop. I looked for a difference between them, but they were identical. My eyes shut just as my lips closed on the tip of the left nipple, and then moved down a little, and then a little further, until the entirety of it was in my mouth. It felt different than it had in my fingers; not smooth and perfectly shaped by a potter's hand, but with tiny crevices across it and rough edges around it. I began sucking on it, like a baby. There was a little shiver in her chest. My lips found the tiny bumps at the base. A slight move by her pushed her

other breast a little closer to my mouth. I abandoned the left nipple
and slid my mouth an inch or two over, until I was hovering over
the other. She tapped my head lightly, and I hesitated another second. I bit down, and the girl's chest bucked a little, and she gave a
muffled cry, and her chest bucked again. She turned to me with her
other breast in her hand and pushed it into my mouth. I bit down
on the nipple. She froze in midair for a moment, then released, and
her breastbone banged into my nose.

WHAT WAS THAT? A scraping sound? Like a heavy object being
dragged across the floor. I close my eyes and listen closely: nothing. Old houses are full of noises. I had checked in the closets and
under the beds, even the fruit cellar around back. Everyone is gone
now. I'm carrying forth alone, and I'm tired. I can see my mother
standing at the kitchen counter in her apron, cutting brightly colored vegetables on a board and humming quietly to herself. Joseph
had been in our kitchen more than once for snacks after a day at
the water. My mother loved to ruffle his thick sandy hair. I don't
remember her, or my father, mentioning his name afterward.

The innocence the boy on the train wears as a cloak doesn't
seem like that to him now; he feels clumsy and awkward and ignorant; but the girl sees it, and it draws her to him. She is used to
boys seeking to devour her in one bite, and in his hesitation she sees
sweetness, perhaps even caring.

I cherish the story of the night on the train, not only for its own
sake, but because it's clear to me now that the telling of it is the
only way to reach the finish line before the dawn.

I turn the light out and listen. Nothing. Through the window I see that night's black canopy has been punctured by a shower of tiny diamonds. Clouds sail beneath the moon, now a whiter shade in the glow of the stars, and cast their own shadows across the lake. There is time left, I think, but not a lot. I wonder, as I have before, what the boy would've been like if he had never lost the story of the detectives at the front door and what had gone before. Once the membrane is breached, there is little to be done. No repair. No healing. For some, the best way is to die before the roiling images burst through. As for me, the boy on the train, or the unsuspecting groom at the wedding ceremony, the future was long ago foretold. My father, in his slacks and summer shirt, came to the door in his usual pleasant attitude, which became grim as he listened to the detective. The first one, I noticed, did not remove his fedora until he had come inside and stood in the foyer with his partner. My mother's face was stricken. She glanced at me, as if she wished she could tell the two men they had made a mistake, there was no boy by that name living here. Neither of the men looked in my direction, as if not wanting to scare me into flight, but I noticed that the lead guy switched to talking to my father. I saw a thin fold of skin, or a scar, beneath his left ear, running down almost to his chin. I lit a filter cigarette with a silver table lighter and tried to listen. Both men were inside now, hats off, held in one or both hands, and now the second one, on the right, with motionless eyes and small ears set too far back on his head, spoke, and in his quiet words I could make out the name of my best friend, David. My heart lightened; David and I had done a lot of shit together, stealing watches from department stores, cartons of cigarettes from grocery stores, even his parents' car in the middle of the night, which we joy-rode around Booneville smoking and bullshitting about stuff we'd done with girls. But that wouldn't account for the look of disgust on my mother's face, or the pain on my father's, or the dull undertone of the detective's voice. I crushed the lousy-tasting weed in a blue glass ashtray on the coffee table. I pulled a Lucky from the flattened pack in my jeans pocket, straightened and plumped it, and lit it. I exhaled and out of habit blew several smoke rings, which charged one after the other to the center of the room, where they hung in a row, until the last one blew through the first and settled down on the couch. The second cop caught it, and he seemed to calculate what sort of attitude they had here. Suddenly, all four of them were looking at me, and the lead detective stepped into the living room. Followed by my mother.

My tough-guy attitude was something I had acquired hanging around the corner drugstore. There was no steel inside, although the girl on the train didn't see that; she thought I knew what I was doing. I wanted to talk to her. Words were how I knew things. Like now, tapping on the keys of this ancient machine, gathering the letters and the silent sounds they represent into some sort of story of the night on the train so I can finally let go. I can't adequately describe the feel of the air as my parents and the two detectives entered the living room, or the sounds as they walked across the carpet, or the sight of their limbs dangling at their sides as they came to a stop, in a semicircle. Maybe there is a little steel, after all, for I remember I was quite determined that I was not going to stand up for the detectives. Neither was I going to stop smoking, although I saw the smaller one with still eyes glance at the Lucky in my hand as if it were some sort of a weapon. So I stayed seated and waited for one of them to say something.

OUR PARENTS' FEAR at the lake house had always been that one of us would hang onto the rope too long and crash on the far bank of the river. It never seemed to occur to them that one of us could be lost when a canoe turned over in the middle of the lake. We could handle canoes; we tipped them over all the time for fun. We were all good swimmers. We jumped and dove off the dock, where the water was well over our head. So, the shock when Joseph drowned out there. I can feel the tightness in my chest. Maybe I did see him in the woody tangle on the water's edge. The purple-veined skin, the staring eyes are suddenly quite vivid.

THE TWO MEN with fedoras? Clear as ice water. My mother said the men were detectives and wanted to talk to me. I stayed in my seat and said nothing, so the two men pulled up chairs across the coffee table from me and sat down. The big one set his gray fedora on the table next to the glass ashtray and reached inside his coat pocket and withdrew a small leather wallet and flipped it open to show a bright gold badge. He said his name, put it back in his jacket, and settled his elbows on his knees. His hands were wide and heavy.

"You smoke?" he said. "You're twelve?"

I lay the butt in the ashtray. My mother began to say something; he lifted a hand to silence her. A few months earlier, my best friend—the one whose name I had heard from the second detective's mouth—and I had almost set the house on fire smoking in a crawl space in the basement; after which my parents gave me permission, begged me, to smoke in the house, in front of them. They even occasionally put a few Luckies in the silver box. The detective's gray eyes were serious. The thing with Judy Pauling in the basement, I thought. The three of us had taken our clothes off, and she had lain on the couch, on her stomach, and my friend and I took turns lying on top of her. Nothing happened. No one talked her into anything. In fact, we set up a date to do it again the next week, at her house, when her folks would be out of town.

I let his question pass. My parents were standing a few feet behind the seated detectives.

"Son, we want to ask you a few questions about your friend David and a man named Willie Benson."

Where was I?

My nose was sore.

"Oh, dear," the girl said, playfully. She reached in her coat pocket and pulled out a handkerchief and dabbed my nose. Red splotches showed on it.

"Sorry," she said.

"All in the line of duty," I responded. She continued dabbing at my nose.

"There," she said, pleased.

Well, that's that, I thought. You've got a story, not *the* story, but still a story, with a bloody nose to top it off. Meanwhile, my pants were still unzipped.

A few stars had surfaced. Lights in a small community shone in the distance. A pickup raced us along the highway. There was not a sound in the car except the clickety-clack of the wheels. Her hand found my dick, now a shadow of its former self. I just wanted to hold her.

"It's all right," I said.

"You think so?" She looked at me, and I saw a glimmer of lust in her eye. She wanted to finish it. She wanted to feel me come. That thought—that me coming turned her on—roused me instantly. She took over, and I lay my head back on the seat in surrender.

A DARK FORM catches my attention. Something flitted in front of the window. Bats. I'd forgotten; they'd been a problem every summer, living in the attic. My mother shrieked and chased them around the house with a broom, always knocking one or two to the floor, which our dog jumped on and tried to eat. I'd thought the bats would have headed south, to Mexico or wherever they went, by now. A couple of them flew across the face of the moon. One bat after another sliced through the reddening streak, leaving the crimson drops to slide down the cut and into the sky. The difference between it happening and me seeing it happen was so slight as to often be irrelevant, except as now when I was trying to sort out myth from truth, to obtain a little peace. The myth could say that the blood of the moon fell into a pool, and the pool had great powers for those who drank of it. Where was the pool? was the enduring question. Men searched their whole lives for it, dying unquenched. Those who found it swore an oath not to reveal its whereabouts, for they would be turned to dust if they did. It wouldn't matter if no one ever saw the moon actually bleed, the crimson drops blacken as they hit the sky, for people wanted to believe in such things. I could write the myth out and not long after it would be accepted not as casual ravings but as archetypal insight by some, the truth by others. And I might come to believe it, as well, for reasons that should be becoming obvious by now. I turn all the stories of my life over and over in my mind and toss them in various bins, depending on the likelihood of their reality. I sometimes switch them around. The story of Judy Pauling ends up in the "very likely" bin most times, although I wouldn't swear to each and every detail. Same with the story of my best friend screwing my wife. Now, Joseph was a different situation. Just because I hadn't thought of him—the drowning—for all these years means nothing. We never returned to the lake after that summer. I hadn't been back until today, and I might not even then have remembered Joseph had it not been for the odd look on the caretaker's face. I know Joseph drowned; whether I saw his body in the woody tangle on the shore is another matter. In most instances, the truth really doesn't matter. I would have split from my wife whether or not my friend fucked her. Joseph was a tall, scrawny kid, but not someone you would try to push around. I liked him, although we didn't hang around a lot. I had a crush on his older sister, which didn't help me in his eyes, although I never even held her hand. Sally. I had forgotten her, as well. She had black hair but the same green eyes as Joseph, her only sibling. I saw her afterward, at a small gathering at their house. She wouldn't look at me.

THE TRUTH OF a few things does matter. But the images always seem to be in shards, never linked, never whole; like the remains of a shipwreck, bits and pieces of which wash ashore over time, as the ocean gives them up. Some might clear for a time, and you think that's how it was, and then the next time it's blurry around the edges, and the blurriness spreads until the scene crumbles and fades like a photographic image taken out of the fixer solution too soon. Or the scenes run awry, the images mix and blend, and never stand in a straight line, where you could say this is the way it happened, never where there is a beginning and an end. It's nothing you can fix by attention, I've learned that. Nothing's ever there completely at the same time, for you to study and arrange in proper order, like a jigsaw puzzle. If you concentrate on the gray fedora, on the words out of the detective's mouth, or your mother's stiff-legged stance, or you remark on the thick tension in the room, in an attempt to move the story forward to the next instant in time, you're going to be disappointed. The first detective reached into his coat pocket and slowly lifted a dark object from it while keeping his eyes on me. It was a black wallet, and it looked familiar. It was thin and had worn edges. The detective held it out in front of me like a dead fish and asked if I'd ever seen it. I looked away.

"No," I said.

The detective waited for me to look back.

"You're sure? You've never seen this before?" I took another look at it. It was my friend's. On the back was the imprint of the rubber he carried in the slot behind the money.

"No," I said.

He knew I was lying; everyone in the room knew I was lying. Carefully, the detective laid the wallet on the glass coffee table.

So, you see the confusion: the look of aversion on Sally's face, the stinking fish wallet on the glass table, my wife's face as my friend was fucking her, the smell of the lake water at the gathering, as if to remind us Joseph had been in the lake overnight, even the crackling hiss of the door opening at the front of the train car.

A dark form in the yellow light was moving down the aisle toward us, touching the top of each seat to steady himself. Maybe heading for the rear door, which was supposed to be locked, but which I knew from experience usually was not. Maybe it was the preppie I had seen on the platform. Blazer, rep tie, penny loafers. Perhaps he had spoken to the girl in the station; maybe he knew her; had done this with her before. I reached for the girl's coat and pulled it up over her shoulders and then up over her head. I peered into the dim orange light. The train rocked to the right, and the face in the aisle picked up a glimmer. It was the woman a few rows behind us, with the crying baby. She couldn't care less about what was going on here. Her eyes passed right over us.

"All clear," I murmured, letting my hand drift down to the girl's hip.

I glance out the oval window and consider the time. The sky seems to be blackening. I close my eyes. Images of violence slip through the loose weave at strange times, like this. After my wedding, I walked my bride from the steps of the church to the waiting

Chevy, being driven by who else but my best friend, the very one whose wallet the lead detective had so forlornly lay on the glass table in front of me, the very one who would later fuck the bride. As he came around the back to open the door, I pictured myself slipping a gleaming ice pick from the inside of my tuxedo jacket and thrusting it smoothly into my bride's back, between her ribs, and then pulling it out so quickly no one could tell. A whuff of air escapes her as she lowers her head, and I realize I'd hit a lung. She glances around, as if a bee had stung her, and her body hesitates a second, and I smile back. Little beads of blood finally begin appearing, one by one, through the tiny hole in the taffeta. It's for that image—the bright crimson on the pure white—that I've done it. It's not a desire to inflict pain, or to punish or humiliate, or even to injure or kill; it was simply a matter of curiosity. The *feeling* as you pulled the pick out, and you would know from the sight of it that life was irrevocably altered, and you couldn't go back to the second before you shot your arm out, when all was light and future and happiness—I wanted to know what that moment felt like. To be free of all responsibility for the rest of my life, to be able to watch it play out like a film, to not give a shit. How can you truly know life without taking one?

So, this murderer comes peeping in on me at moments where I'm blinded by the whiteness of my bride's wedding dress, or Shelley Duvall's smooth neck, and leaves behind an image of a crimson river streaming through the snowy whiteness. There's little to be done about it. In the backseat of the Chevy, my bride turns to me for a kiss, and I oblige.

One time I came a little closer than usual to living out the fantasy. Several years after the wedding, on a vacation, we stayed in a friend's guest cottage in a fishing village on the Maine coast. There were two single beds, one on either side of the room, and the second night, after we'd drunk two bottles of wine, we separated to the individual beds. Laying there, alone in the single bed, I imagined slipping from bed, walking quietly into the kitchen, and picking up the long thin knife I'd used to filet the salmon. I imagined running my finger down the blade, raising a drop of blood, before walking over to where she lay. The urge became so strong as I lay there, listening to her breathe, that I had to mentally paralyze my legs and arms so I couldn't get out of bed and walk to the counter where the knife lay. I felt no hostility toward her; I wasn't angry at her—this was at least five years before the "betrayal." All I really wanted was to experience the shock on her face when she realized what was happening, when she felt the knife release and the blood stream between her breasts and down her stomach, the moment she saw my eyes and every dream of life vanished from her head.

I LEAN FORWARD in my chair. The typewriter seems a forbidding object—cold metal skin, worn gold letters, an array of knobs and levers, a ribbon soaked in ink—for tasks and times such as this. Yet, we are not alone, I know that. The winged creatures creasing the yellow-orange moon, the lingering spirits of the Augusts of my youth, whatever thing is rattling around down below. Perhaps Joseph's father has come back to force his son's name onto my

lips, his image into my eyes. What could I say? Sally, I would like
to know about, but to ask about her would be to ignore Joseph,
to point a finger at the hole where he should have been. She finally
looked at me the afternoon of the wake, I remember. Her eyes
green and cold as the lake water. We left the lake house the night
of the gathering, although it was only the beginning of the second
week of August.

I scan the words on the page on the table to the right of the
typewriter. It seems like the word "wallet" should have two "t"s,
to give it a bit more snap, and I decide I will spell it that way from
now on. I remember working to figure out what the thing meant,
lying there like that. How the detectives got a hold of it, what they
were doing with it here.

"It belongs to your friend David," the detective croaked, leaning a few degrees forward, as if to intimidate me.

The crease in his cheek, running from his left ear over his jawbone, was clearly a scar. What had confused me was how it seemed
to hide in a fold. He caught me staring at it; the scar was like a
prop, I thought; he uses it to distract people, to gain an advantage.
I stubbed out the Lucky in the glass ashtray, glanced at the red and
black bull's-eye on the flattened pack on the table. Three or four
left. I felt myself wrap up, sink inside, deeper, leaving only enough
behind to nod and murmur. I could hang out in this numb space
for a long time, and there was nothing my mother or the cops could
do about it. A few months earlier my mother had become so dis-
turbed over my behavior that she had taken me to a psychologist
in Booneville. I saw him four or five times, and he ran a large tape

recorder on his desk as I told him stories about what a tough guy I was at school. Somebody stole a cigarette from my locker, and I beat him up. Or all the things I had done with girls. I figured he knew I was bullshitting him, but it gave him something to report to my mother. Your youngest son lives in a fantasy world. He has difficulty telling the difference between what he dreams up and what's real. I denied having imaginary friends, but I almost had him convinced that Roy Rogers and his horse Trigger had stayed at my house over last Thanksgiving. Convinced enough that he asked my mother about it after the session.

I STAND UP, and the chair screeches back. The sound zips up my back, as if it were somehow related to the bats winging across the face of the moon or the rattling, scraping noises struggling up from below. A wind has come up; the jagged oak leaves are trembling; the branches are rising and falling, dancing. For a moment the moon seems almost hidden in the stars. I take a step toward the door. The old boards underfoot creak.

Willie Benson. All those years I hadn't heard that name. And now, standing here in the small space of my little warren, the name simply materializes, with no fanfare, as if it really wasn't strange at all. Maybe I could have told you "Willie" if you'd asked. Maybe. But never the last name. The detective had said it, and now that I think about it I remember reading a newspaper article that the guy had gone to jail. So I had known it at one time. David told me Willie could get us girls. Even at twelve, we talked constantly about girls and sex. We listened slack-jawed as one of David's friends told us in detail about how he fucked his sister. We hung around a small engine-repair shop run by a good-looking middle-aged guy who smoked a pipe and delivered mail. He told us about women he screwed on his route. We followed him one Saturday morning. Halfway through his route, he walked up the steps to a small brick duplex, leather mailbag over his shoulder, and was greeted at the top by a young housewife wearing a yellow see-through skirt and a sleeveless top. After a few words, she opened the screen door and he followed her inside. We clocked him at ten minutes. We knew the husband—he worked at a dairy across town.

The fact was, as I've said, we were a little hesitant about the real thing. Now, there was Judy Pauling. She was very quick about everything; she took her panties off, stood there for a second, and we could see something nestled in the hair, but we never got a look beyond that. The thing with her came to an end one summer night when, according to plan, we showed up at her bedroom window with the intent of slipping her out and heading to a park a block away. When we knocked on the glass, she didn't respond, so we knocked louder, and the window finally opened, and her head poked out. "Go away!" she whispered. A male voice barked from inside: "Where's the fucking shotgun?" A large dog started barking. We took off, and I got my leg hung up on the sharp point of a picket on a fence in the backyard and ripped up a piece of flesh pretty good.

THE GIRL ON the train lies imbued in my mind. But if I'm not careful, I could lose her amidst the tumult. The story could wander off

into hiding behind the fading stars of dawn. I sat back down in front
of the typewriter. Underwood. God only knows what else had been
written on the machine: letters and memoirs, scientific papers, short
stories, even poems and diaries. Suicide notes. All the many fingers
who had tapped out the thoughts of their owners on these very keys,
struggling for clarity, beauty, or impact. On the drive up, I pictured
myself sitting at the kitchen table, scribbling away on a pad into the
night. When the caretaker, Joseph's father, had flipped through the
keys on the ring on the front porch, he paused for a moment at the
ones to the basement and the tiny room on the fourth floor, almost
as if he were daring me to use them. The old Underwood had been
sitting here on the table next to a stack of white paper, awaiting me.
I saw that the view from the window down onto the garden and
the stone fence and the water beyond would be perfect. I retrieved
the lamp from the bedroom on the third floor and proceeded to the
room in the attic, which I haven't left since.

THE HEAD OF blonde hair continued rising and falling in my lap
in a steady rhythm. My fingers pressed into the skull. Every time her
head rose I was on the verge of coming. What would happen to us
when it was over? She rested her head on my lap, eyes closed, and
massaged my dick just enough to keep it stiff. Like this, through the
dark night we would speed, rocking back and forth, connected by
need and spirit and the steady click-clacking of steel on steel.

The rear door hissed open, and the click-clacking rose to a
scream and the cold air whooshed in. You could hear the door try
to close, and then jerk back open, meaning someone was standing

in the doorway, hesitating on whether to go on out. The baby
started crying, and I wondered if the mother was going to throw it
off the back of the train. The girl was so still I guessed she might
have fallen asleep.

SOMETIMES IT SEEMS all my life I've been dragging my story
behind me like a heavy, unseen stone. But tonight I am completely
awake, and I am beginning to worry about the fleeting darkness.
Everything stirs in my head. Rattling sounds, now more insistent,
from below shiver up the boards and into my bones. The sounds
fade gradually, like the end of a song. I can smell the ink on the
page. If I were to rise and open the window, I could reach out and
touch the moon, which seems in the past hour to have assumed
a larger, more commanding presence in the sky, although now I
notice a micro-thin layer of white clouds is sliding beneath it, scat-
tering its light. After that night in the bedroom, I never made love
to a woman without an image of my wife and best friend showing
up on the screen. I never stuck her, either with a blade or a pick,
or I wouldn't be sitting here at this table, but I have no doubt the
image of her in my mind as she sees her blood on the tip of the ice
pick is what she would have looked like had I done it. A stunning
moment of completion.

And, of course, images of the girl on the train; but never before
this moment have I tried to put them in chronological order, to tell
the story from beginning to end. Why now? you might ask. I have
no answer. Coming here, after forty-some years, in the fall of the
year, on a moonlit night, with no memory of Joseph or the canoe,

or even his lovely sister. I can feel the icy water now, as it must have felt to him as he slipped under, the burn as it entered his nose. His head went down, then popped up, then went down again, and up again, and then down, and not up again. A few words the first time, then nothing, gasping and spitting. What was wrong with him? He knew how to swim. Cramps. That's what he was saying. Cramps. What was he doing way out in the middle of the lake where no one could hear him? Probably on his way to the Girl Scout camp on the other side. I had paddled over there and back with him a few days before. These images are so clear now, so frightening, that I believe them; they've been hanging around this old house all these years like dust motes or faded photographs, and my presence brings them back to life. The life jackets were bright orange, and there were always two in every canoe. I remember now, it began as a calm day on the water. We were swimming races between the docks on either side of the mouth of the river earlier in the morning and there wasn't a ripple. Sally was there, in a red bathing suit, black hair piled under a cap, but still pretty. She blew the starting whistle and declared the winners. When someone argued with her over a call she took off her cap, bent over the water, and talked into his face, and the boys peeked for a view of her tits, which were nice. The lake water was so still that morning the sun pooled lazily on it, and clouds of tiny bugs skimmed its surface.

Now I see quite clearly: Joseph is standing by the canoe trying to cajole someone into paddling to the Girl Scout camp with him. He's wearing black trunks with a red sea horse on the left leg. His yellow hair pokes out in all directions like straw. Sally watches with little interest. Other boys are tempted to grab a paddle, but it's against the rules. When I went a week earlier, it took a lot longer to get there than he said. I talked with a girl at the camp for a while. I can't think of her name, but I remember she had red hair, worked in the camp kitchen, and lived in town. The wind had picked up a little on the way back across the lake, and it was pushing us sideways by the time we reached the shore. I can see Joseph standing up in the canoe as it slid up on the beach, showing off. That was it for me. Fifteen feet out and you were in over your head, and in the middle of the lake the water was over fifty feet deep and cold enough to freeze your heart in an instant.

I picture him stepping in, settling on the rear seat, and reaching for the paddle. He's not wearing a life jacket. Maybe there is one in the canoe and he put it on as he paddled out, but at that moment his skinny, tough frame is unencumbered. The rest of us left the beach to play on the tire swing, and I remember Sally was no more concerned than the rest of us. She grabbed the tire, ran a couple of steps, and swung out over the water. I can see the crack in the bottom of her suit as she kicks her legs; I can hear her scream as she let go, see the water rise and dance in the sunlight as she hit.

LOOKING OUT THE window, at the streak of moonlight on the water, and the sudden appearance of ghostly dark clouds, I feel like I'm the captain of the ship, in the pilot house, guiding it confidently through the rough seas of the night. There's nothing to fear anymore; I worry only that time will defeat me, although the darkness beyond the moon seems to be holding. As for the images of Joseph in the canoe? Sally on the tire swing? They come from somewhere, don't they? The mind needs a story, and it sorts and keeps and discards as a narrative emerges, and so one embraces the current version at one's peril, but when there is nothing left to defend, to keep put together for, when you've quit waiting to get somewhere, it seems to me the story might begin to bear a strong resemblance to what actually happened; and it also seems to me that these images should be entitled to a little more weight than usual since they have appeared from nowhere, after so many years of not thinking of Joseph—not just his death, but anything about him. That, and the vividness of them, although the images of my wife with a bloody ice pick wedged in the ribs of her white wedding dress are just as vivid. Could we have played on the swing, watched Sally spin off into the sky, before Joseph paddled off across the water? Yes. Absolutely. In fact, now I'm sure that it was after lunch that he left in the canoe.

I walk over to the door and twist the bolt. The metallic sound strikes my skull. You push too hard on this stuff and you get nowhere. I don't remember Joseph actually paddling off, for example; I just remember that he wasn't there when it was time to go home. I don't remember the lead detective ever putting the wallett back in his pocket. Of course I denied knowing Willie Benson. If I didn't recognize the wallett, I couldn't recognize the name Willie Benson.

"You're not supposed to hang around with David Wright."

My mother's voice, reeking with accusation and shame, split the silence. The first detective glanced up at her. My father looked out the window. I didn't have many friends, and those I did have were troublemakers like me, living on the outside of the circle. David's reputation in Booneville was even worse than mine, and he knew characters way outside the circle. One day he came into the repair shop and began telling me about Willie. The man knew where to get girls, he said. We had talked about such a thing endlessly, dreamed about it, tried to imagine what a real pussy would feel like. It wasn't so much about fucking as it was crossing the line from fantasy into reality, to actually *touch a girl there*. David was adamant; his excitement was catching. Have you done it? I asked. No, but he trusted Willie to find the girls. He would arrange for a whore at the state fair, or one of the girls working out of the Booneville Hotel. The two of us went out the back and sat on the step, where we could spit and smoke, and David went on about it, and I sat and listened.

Funny, now I can remember the red pack of tall Pall Malls that David pulled from his shirt pocket, how he shook the pack hard once and a single weed popped out. I took it and thwacked it several times on the side of the Zippo (the same one I would carry on the train a couple of years later, shiny as silver, with the Marine Corps emblem on one side). I lit my weed first, then his.

David let the smoke drift out of his mouth and then pulled it up into his nostrils. We shunned the new filtered cigarettes, except for Kools, which I stole by the pack from the carton my parents kept in a kitchen drawer. We talked some more about Willie and girls, and even then I felt there was something screwy. Why would a grown man want to get a girl for a couple of kids? David mentioned giving him a few bucks, but I didn't buy it. What about Judy Pauling? I asked. No good, he said. Her father had figured out what was going on and kept her on ice.

We sat there for an hour, smoking and spitting and talking about the girl Willie was going to get for us. The pavement in front of us got so wet it hissed when you tossed a butt on it. The screen door opened, and the postman appeared. He told us to clean up the mess.

I HOLD MY hand up to the night sky and spread my fingers wide until the moon catches between the knuckles of the second and third digit. The moon seems to have filled up a little, as if someone had poured molten light into it. I squeeze gently until the orb flattens out a little. I relax my fingers, and it springs back into shape. The blood streaks on it are gone. The moon is pure and pretty as the first night it shone. My mother's voice reverberates in my bones. I knew by then what it was about; the only way to survive this scene was to stay hidden. Once I said yes or no or maybe, I was screwed. I shook my head at another question. I hadn't really done anything, after all, just gone along for the ride and watched the scene play out. The second detective, with the eyes that didn't move, and the small ears stuck low and back on his head, picked up the wallett and opened it. There was a little pocket with a snap on it for change. Behind a piece of scratched plastic was a photograph. It was of David, with the usual smirk on his face, the flattop with the lock curled over his forehead.

"You know him?" The guy's voice was surprisingly deep, like a radio announcer's.

I nodded.

"Who is it?"

I peered closely.

He took the picture out of its case and held it up to me.

"David Wright?"

I nodded. He lay the picture down on the glass table and opened the last fold in the wallett, as if to extract something else. He pulled out a small photo. It was a girl, with blonde hair, a forced smile. Judy Pauling.

"You know her?"

I shook my head. He lay it down on the table, next to the picture of David. I had misread the situation; this *was* about Judy. Her father had beaten it out of her, the stuff in the basement. But the cop had mentioned Willie. Willie and Judy did not go together. Maybe a photo of Willie was coming out next. I pictured him: slight, short, balding, small black eyes in a sallow face. The three of us met outside a drugstore on the main street of Booneville early one afternoon. David and I stood there for half an hour before he showed up. We stepped under an awning, and he explained that he had arranged for a girl from the fair grounds to meet us at his apartment. Her name was Janice. Half an hour apiece, and wouldn't cost us a thing. He kept glancing around as he talked. Suddenly, he was gone. Behind us not twenty yards stood the postman. He had followed us, and Willie had spotted him and figured him for a cop. The postman gave us a ride back to the shop in exchange for a promise to stay away from Willie.

I PUNCH THE keys on the Underwood in a vain attempt to describe the feeling of that night on the train. No other time with a woman came close to it. Surely I was to blame for that. I see myself as chasing that sensation the rest of my life, always slightly on the run, scared to come to a complete stop for fear of what might overrun me, and drop me. Sometimes, usually when booze or drugs were part of the mix, the barriers to impulse gave way, like the night of my best friend's wedding party, some five years after I'd caught him and my wife together, when all supposedly had been forgiven and everyone, all three of us, had moved on. I was standing on the makeshift stage at the resort outside of Montego Bay giving the best man's speech, rambling on about what a remarkable couple they made, and suddenly the bullshit of it all made me hesitate just long enough for the familiar scene of the two of them fucking to slip through the netting. I looked around for my former wife in the wedding party, and when I spotted her sitting with the bride's parents, a half-empty rum drink in front of her, blonde hair pulled back into a long ponytail, smiling up at me, I raised my glass. "Finally, I'd like to thank David for fucking my wife. In the ass, I might add. I'm looking forward to returning the favor. Cheers!"

It was one of my favorite scenes and pretty out of character for me. Particularly since their cheating had never really bothered me. Was I really that articulate? Was the look on the bride's face as ghastly frozen as I see it now? Did I really slam the champagne and march happily off the stage? I should have felt bad, of course—Julie, the bride, had done nothing to me—but I didn't. A funny thing was, my former wife came to my room a few hours later in her underwear, drunk, and demanded that I fuck her. I think I did, for old times' sake, or to get a final laugh on David, but I couldn't swear to it.

I TRY TO refocus on the page in front of me, the round keys with the letters on them, but the distractions are beginning to take over; I'm losing the girl on the train; and time is thinning out. The stars surrounding the moon now have grown sharper, like there is fire on the edges. The wind ticks a small branch against the window, and it plays against the rattling and scraping noises from down below. The whole night is a concert, a play, of beauty and spirit. It's like this at the end, I think. A purple haze drifts across the face of the moon. Or perhaps it's always been like this, I just haven't seen it.

I see the problem now. The rods of the "t" and "h" keys have collided in mid-stroke and are stuck together. I stand and wobble a little. I reach in, twist the rods apart, and they fall easily back into place. I glance at the ribbon. It seems fat enough on the spool. The paper on the left is still stacked high. I punch a capital "T" for train. The conductor wears the same wire-rimmed spectacles as the second detective, the one with the still eyes and small ears. He massages the edge of the wallett like some sort of talisman. He addresses me, but I can't hear his voice, only feel his eyes. It will go on, until I talk. But why are they here, if David didn't send them? Maybe the weasel Willie ratted us out. I get it. They found David's wallett in Willie's room. But then, why aren't they talking to David? I reach for my Luckies on the edge of the table, but the first detective flops a fat finger on the pack, pinning it down. Our eyes lock. He wins.

I punch a key again. If I'm not more attentive, the girl will leave. I need her here with me until the stars begin to fade and I proceed to finish the long corrugated story of my life. The train, I remember, hurtled through the blackness like it could jump the tracks and shoot over the curvature of the earth. Inside it, with me, was this girl, her head on my chest, and beyond this there was nothing.

She sat up. I slipped my hand from beneath her sweater. I began twisting my pants around and fumbling for the zipper, when she said, "I'll be right back." She straightened her clothes and ran her fingers through her hair. She patted my cheek, stood, and stepped into the aisle.

I watched her walk toward the light at the end of the car, her hips swaying provocatively. The guys at school will never believe me, not that I would tell them. I glanced out the window. We were passing under a tall bridge, and the cars on it looked like they were magnets stuck in the sky. In spite of what the girl said, I feared she'd come back all fixed up with a new attitude. We'd talk, and eventually she would nod off, and there I'd sit basically alone, wide awake, until the train pulled into the Chicago station in the early light. Then there'd be a few words of affection, a brief kiss, and the story would be over. I could finish it in my mind and let that version become the truth. I was thinking that might not be such a bad ending, really, when suddenly the clickety-clack took on a slightly hollow sound. I looked out the window and realized we were on a high bridge, crossing over a wide river. Below us in the water were long thin dark shapes with red lights at either end. The whistle blew two long cries, and the train began to slow. The carriage jerked and slowed further. Maybe the rails ahead were torn up. What if the train pitched to one side and fell down into the water? We'd all drown. I could really use a weed. I looked over at my old seat; the pack of Luckies was sitting on top of the sack with the dirty magazine, like someone had helped themselves. Which meant the Zippo could be gone. I glanced up the aisle—no sign of her. The train jerked again, the brakes squealed, and we slowed almost to a stop. Still no one stirred. I zipped myself up and stepped across the aisle, found the lone weed and the Zippo on the seat, just where I'd left them. A long time ago, it seemed. Before the girl. I stuck the Luckies in the sack and glanced at the cover of the magazine: a brunette in panties and bra, looking over her shoulder at me. I made my way to the back of the car. The crumpled forms on the seat were fast asleep, unbothered by the screeching of metal on metal, by the fact that we hung suspended in the air over a dark wide river. I punched the button on the door, it hissed and slid open. I walked a few steps onto the metal platform and into the cold night air. The wooden ties stuck out only a few feet beyond the tracks; the struts of the bridge itself were made of wood. Metal against wood. Two steps and I was off the train; another and I was in the air. The train jerked to a complete stop, knocking me back into the door. I leaned out and looked ahead; the entire train was on the bridge; I saw the struts beneath us crumpling like toothpicks from the steel weight. At the first cracking, I would jump free from the train, fold up into a cannonball, and spin down. Praying to miss a boat.

On the other side of the river were the lights of a small town, huddled on the banks. Behind us, blackness. I stuck the Lucky between my lips, clinked open the Zippo, cupped my hand around it, and struck the wheel with my thumb. The flame bent toward me. The first pull burnt my lungs. The smoke swirled off into the stars. I held the cigarette between thumb and forefinger and waited for the cracking sounds beneath me. I took another drag. The door hissed behind me, and I felt a presence.

"Hi."

It was the girl. She was taller than I thought.

"What are you doing out here?" she asked. Before I could answer, she glanced down at the river and asked, "Are you going to jump?"

"No," I said.

"Why are we stopped?"

I shrugged. I felt a blast of desire. My hand rose and touched her neck. I leaned in to kiss her and felt the heat from her lips. After a few seconds, she pulled back. She was trembling. Her eyes held onto me. The sadness was gone and something else was there.

I've never been able to put words to that look, and I'm not doing much better now. I can say the moment expanded into hours, yet lasted only a second. In her eyes, beyond the beauty and the heat, beyond the sadness, was a need so deep it held me fast in place. There was for an instant a communion of trust and belief, of gaining freedom from some unseen devils. Her eyes were an invitation. Her trembling hand touched mine. I willed my hand to turn and encompass it and hold it tightly. Instead I reached for the railing. I glanced away for a second, at the lights on the far edge of the river.

I couldn't have understood it at the time, I think now, as the keys strike the paper. She did, though. She saw it. She had made an offering, and I had fled. But, on my behalf, I have to say giving into her eyes felt scarier than jumping off the platform into the river.

I feel it now, in my fingertips, her trembling, and I believe it is spreading into the rods and the keys, for the letters are smudged and uneven. I lift my hands, hold them in the air, then seek to force them down onto the keys to continue banging out the story and the scene as if I had grasped her hand and gone with her, wherever she led.

There is no sound, I realize. Not the ticking on the window, not the rattling from below, not even my own breathing. Absolute stillness. I listen harder, then stand up to hear the chair scrape. Nothing. I twist the roller to hear the clicking. I see the sounds, but I hear nothing. Complete silence. The branches are knocking silently against the window. I say Joseph's name, but nothing sounds. I say it again, louder, "Joseph!" and still nothing. "Motherfucker." I bang my knuckles on the desk. I bang them again, and listen hard. I snap my fingers, I whistle. Has the world gone silent? I walk to the door, open it, and poke my head into the darkness. Nothing. I needed to go down the stairs, to the bathroom, but not in a sound-less space. Whatever was rattling and scraping down there might be hanging around at the bottom of the stairs. The thought brings me to panic. I need to hear something, anything. A silent world is unbearable; it is noise that keeps you glued together, keeps the bor-ders secure, the floors and ceilings in place. There must be a switch to flip. I kick the door shut. I turn back into the room. I inhale a large breath, and on the exhale hum soundlessly "row, row, row

your boat, gently down the stream." I close my eyes, snap them
open. My hands are someone else's, thick and bulky, like a farm-
er's. I spread the fingers wide, see a shakiness, like leaves in a wind.
I press them onto the table, hard, until the trembling stops. You
don't suddenly go deaf, I think; it's some sort of a hysterical reaction. I walk to the window. Lift the small, rusted latch on the right
edge of the oval, swing the window out. The night seems sharp
and clear, scrubbed free of the grime of perception. The branches
framing the scene, black and spindly, seem tightly woven together
as if by an overly industrious spider. The moon has turned a bright
white and skimmed a little closer to the house. I can see the hatch
marks of the bats on the surface quite clearly now. I reach out to
touch the very edge. The almost-round orb holds perfectly still, until
an icy tingle touches my fingertips. Suddenly, I see a million years
back into the universe, a depth beyond imagination, as if I were
sailing into the timeless glitter of the ancient, boundless heavens.
The sense of isolation vanishes; whichever way I turn are endless
dimensions of stars. The dark rim of the moon glows orange, until
it finally catches fire, and the entire orb begins a slow spin forward.
The universe is silence, I realize; the stars don't whir as they sail on
their paths; the planets hurl soundlessly through space. It's neither
cold nor hot out there, neither good nor bad, full nor empty. I feel
a searing peace. A tremendous wave of gratitude overcomes me,
and my eyes well up. Knowing is a false God. Understanding a
ruse. Feel yourself a member of the universe, properly belonging, as
much as a star or a galaxy, with all the rights and privileges pertain-
ing thereto, and you will be free because you will know once and

for all that nothing matters. You can live that feeling as you walk silently through the garden and climb the stone wall, and standing there, tall and straight, perusing the curvature of the universe and the mighty wave of stars overhead, tipping, tipping, ever so slightly forward, until your balance is gone, and forward you tumble into space. Not Joseph, or the detective, or Willie Benson, or David, or the look in my mother's eye, or even the girl on the train, goes with you. Shrug your shoulders and it will all fall away like a cloak. Without the sound of the wind, or your cry, you will feel nothing as your form dissembles and your spirit flutters off. A soul at peace in the smooth lake at the end of the path. Clarity is an illusion. And a cruel one at that.

A puff of air brushes my cheek. A touch. The girl on the train. My eyes close. So she is alive, somewhere, existing in the same moment under the same godless heavens. I shake my head. My moment of stillness and silence is over. I see that the story needs to be finished before anyone, even the girl on the train, finds peace. As I am closing the window, I hear a loud tap, the sound of a key on paper. I say the girl's name aloud. I've known it all these years. It's lain like a crumpled flower somewhere in the fecund subconscious.

THE PROFESSOR

T'S TIME TO venture forth from my little warren. I need descend only one flight of stairs, to the bathroom in the middle of the hall. I think of the kitchen, but I'm neither hungry nor thirsty, and I'm not sure how many lights work. The rattling sound most certainly came from the kitchen, although the last time it seemed a little louder, a little closer, perhaps at the bottom of the stairs. I spot a broken stave leaning in a far corner. I walk over and pick it up. I swing at an imaginary animal scurrying across the floor, squeaking and belching, and catch it in the head as it leaps. It drops in a broken heap. I see I've caught a splinter in the web between my first two fingers, and blood has oozed onto my palm. Not good, if the thing is a blood seeker. I whack it in the head a couple more times, let the stave fall to the floor.

Leaving the room might bring me around a little, but I dare not lose that elusive linear sense necessary to tell the story. Why peace can only come with understanding I don't know. Perhaps in the end I'll get that as well. I kick the chair with my foot. The girl on the train—so beautiful, so desperate, now floats free in my head, not in reproach but in yearning. What I wouldn't give to change that story, to hold her hand and turn to her rather than away, into the night. You couldn't handle it, I think. The point above all is to stay put together, isn't it? What good can come if you end up scattered in pieces on the floor, a puppet whose strings have been cut? So you fuck up, so you're on the run, so that's life for most people. A little wisdom, late to come in life, brought you here, at last, and for that you should feel a little gratitude. Awaiting you now is the rest of the night on the train with the girl.

When I sit down to resume typing I notice a bloody smear on the stack of fresh paper. I insert the sheet into the machine and spin the roller, until the top of the smear is right where the key hits. I tap out letters to see the effect: My second wife. Sally. Joseph. Blood tells the story, doesn't it? I lick my palm. The images roil in my head, stimulated and freed up by the taste. I type the girl's name into the red. It's a stunning sight: Her name in blood. Next to Joseph, like they belonged together. What had become of them? Joseph had screeched to a breathless halt, while the two of us, the girl and I, sailed on. She struggled and fought and loved and lost and had grown so disconsolate by middle age that she let herself go so no man would want her. To no avail, though. Every fucked-up male was drawn to her. The need to take a life, to see someone's blood flow from their corpus, to know the person's very cessation of being resulted from a decision occurring in my brain, flowing out through my hands, abated somewhat as I grew older, but never completely. I type Willie's name into the blood next to the girl's. It's obscene in a lovely way. I strike him through, and then type him in again, not so close this time. David arranged another meeting with Willie, again on the assurance that this time he would get us a girl. I remember the wet July heat boiling up from the summer sidewalk as we walked the few blocks to the edge of downtown where he lived in a run-down two-story yellow brick apartment building, the type found in every town over a few thousand, for drifters, ex-cons, any sort of misfit. Although I wondered how this guy could manage a girl for us, the idea of walking away never really materialized. My bike was locked up in front of the drug store only a few blocks away.

A cold blast of air swept up from the river. The train jerked back, and then slipped forward, screeching and creaking, wobbling back and forth. I looked around for the girl, but she'd gone back inside. Given up on me, I thought, which was probably just as well. In those few moments I had felt the constraints of the involvement, the pressure in her eyes. Now I could ride with the Ghost Riders across the devil's endless sky, hook back up with the train bandits in their hideout in a distant canyon. The train began to roll a little faster, and the lights of the little town on the far edge of the river grew brighter, and I wondered how many people in the houses there were eating or watching TV or sleeping. I wondered why I still felt nothing, despite the bitter wind. I stood there until the train was over the bridge and the clickety-clack sound returned to normal. Finally, I felt the chill of the night invade my bones. I punched the button for the door. Shivering, I hunched my shoulders and pushed in, only to have the door close on its own and catch me in the chest, pinning me to the frame, half in and half out. I pushed against it, but it only jammed harder. I flung around for the button, but my frozen hands could feel nothing. Suddenly the door snapped open, and there stood the girl. She had been waiting for me. "You poor thing," she said and wrapped me up in her arms. She held me like that, moving her arms gently up and down my back. She lifted my chin, wiped the moisture from the corner of my eyes, and kissed me. She pressed her whole body into me. She led me back to her seat and motioned for me to sit in the chair by the widow. I reached for her, but she pressed my arms down. "Trust me," she said. I lay my head back and forced an exhale.

Her hands slid down and undid my belt and shot the zipper down. In the midst of the struggle I had forgotten about my dick, and now I could feel nothing of it. I flexed it, but still nothing. Frozen solid. Her hand slipped beneath my underwear. Suddenly, there it was. She leaned in to kiss me, and I pulled her in until our lips were smashed together. I found her tongue and sucked until most of it was in my mouth. She pulled my dick all the way out of my pants, and I could see by the way she looked at it that what was coming wasn't another blow job. She held it lightly, turned in her seat and shifted a thigh over me. "Jesus," I whispered. She sat straight up, and I held my breath as my dick disappeared under her skirt.

I could feel the heat of her. She tossed a wave of hair off her shoulder. I fought back the impulse to thrust up into her. Her hands pressed down on my shoulders. I slipped my hands under her skirt and placed them on her thighs, and allowed them to slip up to just about where her panties would be. Her look told me not a millimeter further.

I STAND UP abruptly. The scrape of the chair on the floor is the howl of an angry banshee. I see the wooden canoe, twisting in the waves, and realize I can't remember what happened to it, if it finally floated ashore, or somebody pulled it out. It was ours, I remember now. Our dad had bought it at the end of the previous summer, and we had hauled it here strapped on top of our station wagon. Our name was painted on the green bow in white letters. It carried two paddles and two life vests. I see a vest lying on the sand where Joseph had tossed it. Bright orange. It would have brought him back, and all this suffering would have been avoided. Just because you wanted to impress the girls. You had them anyway; they loved you for your carefree arrogance. We didn't look for our canoe. As I said, we left the day after the reception and never came back.

The bathroom is in the middle of the hall, next to my old room. I have only to walk down the stairs, unlock the door, and it's a few steps on my left. I hesitate to leave my warren, and not just because of the strange sounds coming from below. It's more that I feel content in here, firmly in the spell of the images of the past, as unsettling and untrustworthy as they are. I have very few possessions left; I'd disposed of most of what I owned over the past couple of months, except my car, a green and white 1956 Chevy Bel Air convertible, which I said in a note on the breakfast table should go to my second wife. She liked to fuck in the backseat of the car at outdoor theaters, top down. Her goal was to screw under the stars in fifteen different theaters, and we eventually made it at the Night Vue Drive-In on the outskirts of Council Bluffs. We were together five years. She was the cello teacher in the college conservatory and played first position in the Des Moines Symphony. She liked to show me how she could masturbate with her bow, playing the Ninth on her clitoris, and coming in a long screech in the tumultuous finish of the fourth movement. One spring morning we were drinking coffee at the breakfast table, a light spring breeze raising the curtains, and she said we were over. I nodded, and she got up and packed her instrument and a few things and was gone by noon.

Without David there would have been no Willie Benson, and without Willie Benson there would have been no detectives, no fedoras on the glass coffee table. David could talk his way out of whatever he did, by getting you to see how it made such perfect sense in his head. He denied having fucked my first wife, other than the night I caught them, and I had believed him, although she later confessed otherwise. Just like he denied having given the cops my name, and I let it go.

I'm not an angry person. Nothing burns in my gut. I seek only a peaceful finish; but perhaps peace comes if you no longer struggle for it, if you give up the effort of trying to keep all the pieces in place, the wires hooked up, and let the world stream through you as it will. A movement catches the corner of my eye; the knob on the door turns, ever so slightly. I stare at it. No one could get up the creaky stairs without me hearing them. No person, anyway. Who else could turn it? A raccoon, with its tiny black leathery fingers? I walk to the door. I twist the knob and jerk the door open. Nothing, although I can't see to the bottom of the stairs, where something could be crouching. I flip the light switch. Nothing. Flip it back. It had worked earlier. I remember the strange shadow cast by the hanging bulb on the walls. I flip the switch rapidly. "Fuck you," I call out. There is a small bolt on the door at the bottom of the stairs. The stairs creak under my weight. At the bottom stair, I see that the bolt has been pulled back. I clearly remember jamming the thing into the notch, and then checking it. I run the scene backward in my head. I twist the knob and listen. I push the door open, and there is a clicking, as if something is running off. Joseph had a large black lab, I remember. "Joseph," I whisper, and then again, a little bit louder. "Joseph!" Dead silence. "I'm sorry," I say. Moonlight is slicing in through a window at the end of the hall. I see the door to my old room; across from it is the door to the bathroom. Something might be waiting in the doorway. Fuck it, I think. I don't have to pee anymore. I step back, pull the door shut, and toss the tiny bolt into the slot. I hold still and listen. I ascend the stairs slowly, and stop and listen again at the top.

I return to the table. The stack of paper next to the Underwood is an inch high, yet the story is not half finished. I've never mentioned the girl on the train to a soul, until now. I miss her, yet I can feel her with me, here, tonight. I read back my last few lines, where she swings her leg over me and prepares to settle down on my dick, which is on edge from the wet heat of her. She leaned over, placed her hands on my shoulders, and kissed me. "Ready?" she whispers. I nod, and I feel her pussy brush over me, and then brush back. I wanted to touch it. She tilted her head back, closed her eyes, and lowered herself. I moved my hands slightly up her thighs until I could feel her bottom flattening a little on my thighs. I squeezed it lightly. The girl held me gently inside her. The sensation rolled up through me like a rough tide. Suddenly, still as a scarecrow, she squeezed me gently from the underside. I jerked involuntarily.

"Hey," she said.

Her face was blurry, but there was a hint of a smile on it. I could feel a powerful thrust building inside me.

"Hold still," she whispered. "Very still. We're OK."

WELL, NOW THAT I think about it, I might have seen the girl once again, after our night on the train, although the memory has until the last few minutes lain dormant as a walnut buried deep in the frozen Midwest countryside. I was a professor at City College in Booneville. I'd published a collection of short stories and one novel, the last about a philosophy professor at a major university who became a killer. In the novel, entitled *The Professor*, the teacher had developed his own peculiar theory of nature and the human experience. Research had convinced him that humans, like other animals, were essentially amoral. They behave in their perceived best interest 100 percent of the time. The only reason humans conform their behavior to social norms, like not stealing or committing murder, is that it's in their perceived best interests to do so. Given the right situation, we will all commit murder, without hesitation—in defense of self, or others, or even country. Importantly, the Professor believed that mistakes in perception of self-interest could not be held to be the fault of the individual. If a man felt it necessary to rob a bank to survive, that perception and the impulse behind it were not of his own making. Punish him, if you will, for the best interest of society, but be honest about judging him morally for what he did. Was he involved in the construction of his own personality? Did he design himself to lack impulse control? A conscience? He did what he did because he was who he was.

The Professor was able to shift himself into neutral, from where he could see everything clearly and intimately for what it was. Late one night he caught his wife in the act with his neighbor, in the hammock in their backyard. The next night he cut her throat with a straight razor while she lay asleep in their bed. A few hours later, after organizing his writings, he called the police and turned himself in. He defended himself at trial, was convicted and sentenced to death. *The Professor* caused quite a stir on campus and pissed off my feminist colleagues since they saw the novel as proposing a moral justification for murdering a woman because of her unfaithfulness. Which really wasn't the point at all.

I was walking down the hall of the liberal arts building on campus when I imagined I saw the girl. She was probably twenty feet ahead of me as we descended the wide steps in front of the main building, which opened onto the campus. She turned slightly, as if she sensed I was there. I saw in the face the same look of sensuality and mystery, sadness, although now it lacked the softness of youth. She had a leather bag over her shoulder and was wearing high heels. For a second our eyes touched. She smiled faintly, then looked away. She reached the bottom of the steps and disappeared quickly in the crowd. If it was her, which now I don't think it was, I understand why she hurried off; she knew, as I knew, that the treasure of that night lay in its submersion in the past. The present would interrupt the story and perhaps destabilize it. The narratives of people's lives are what hold them together. Crazy people are those whose narratives have fallen apart, leaving them in chaos. If the story of your life has played out, like mine has, and you'd care to write the end of it, then you do something like I'm doing. You sever yourself from the future, in hopes of finding a final, more enlightened present.

Against the wall, a few feet away, sits my briefcase. Leather, with a strap and buckle, fat at the bottom. Battered from years of lugging books and papers around campus. I'd finally left the college five years ago, when the evident dishonesty in the pursuit of knowledge had become intolerable.

The briefcase has a dark splotch on the leather flap that I don't remember. Like something viscous had spilled on it. I tilt the lamp in its direction; it's seeped into the leather, whatever it is.

David had moved back to Booneville when his father died and took over his commercial printing business. The local paper occasionally ran pictures of him, the lock of hair, now gray, still falling provocatively over his forehead, the same half-ass smirk on his face.

A heavy cloud is passing in front of the moon. I walk to the window and see that the garden is now lost in the shadow. As the cloud drifts by, the shadow lifts. Now I can see in the garden the beauty of what had been; a tangle of vines of faded roses climbing and descending the stone wall in wild profusion.

I feel a twinge of panic. This wandering about in the darkness, while somewhat interesting, will waste the remains of my life. I turn away from the heavens, from the garden below, flick the light back on, and return to my seat. The typewriter has grown cold in my absence. I twist the lamp head to face the paper in the machine. I see the names typed in blood. I add "fedora," because I never heard the detectives' names. They pressed me hard, back and forth, occasionally glancing up at my parents as if to say we can't get anywhere if your son keeps lying. They picked up the wallett, opened it, leaving the head shots of David and Judy Pauling next to each other on the glass table, as if their flat stares might shake me up. "Fedora" doesn't fit within the smear, so I twist the knob and retype it in the middle of the stain a line lower. I was on the verge of pointing the finger at David, but I knew I was dead if I gave the detectives the slightest opening. Everything *had* been his fucking idea. When we had met Willie the second time and he suggested we go to his room, where the girl would supposedly meet us, I hesitated. David took me aside and told me Willie had introduced him to the girl the day before and she was a beautiful redhead with great tits and willing to do anything. The images in my head overwhelmed my skepticism, but I remember asking Willie if we couldn't first meet the girl outside the drugstore. He said she worked at the state fair, but would meet us at his room in half an hour. Gina. I should have walked away right then.

The first detective must have sensed my weakness, because he leaned forward, tried to be casual and sincere at the same time, and said nothing would happen to me, it was Willie they were after. He knew I was lying, but didn't want to have to report me for it. His eyes tried to pin me, and I hesitated, then I caught the glisten of the scar on his face, running like a river from the lobe of ear across his cheek and to the edge of his chin, and was within an instant of asking him how he got it, when he dropped his hand hard on the table.

I jumped, and saw from the corner of my eye that my parents also jumped. Both detectives sat stock still. The voice of the second detective, with the flat eyes, said, "You were in Willie's room, weren't you? With David Wright."

My mother dropped her head.

I could remember quite clearly the two-block walk on the hot sidewalk to the seedy part of town. I walked behind the two of them, past small stucco houses with weed-filled yards and abandoned corner gas stations and old taverns with faded neon signs hanging askew over the front door. I could smell the meatpacking plant across the viaduct. I willed myself to turn around and walk back to the drugstore, but I couldn't. The paint on the front door of the building was peeling. As Willie pulled the door open, I caught the eye of an elderly woman in the second-story window. I could feel sweat on the back of my neck. Willie held the door for me, and I knew it was my last chance. His thin lips disappeared in his oily smile.

"No," I replied to the cop.

He began rubbing the knuckles on his left hand. Staring at me. I flipped open the top of the silver cigarette case and extricated a filter. He twitched like he was going to grab it from my hand, and I sat back immediately, out of his way. Problem was, the lighter was still on the table. My father turned and left the room. My mother glanced at him, then called his name. He had a golf game every Saturday morning. This would really piss her off. She called his name again, more annoyed, and swirled from the room. The second detective, with the small ears too far back, owner of the brown fedora—it had a red feather in the band, I see now—reached for the lighter, lifted it, leaned forward, and punched it. I hesitated. He pushed it out a little further, and the flame bent back. I finally lit the weed. It was tasteless after the Lucky, but I sat back and exhaled. I held the cigarette between two fingers, like an adult. I felt saliva collect under my tongue.

"We know about Judy Pauling," the flat-eyed cop said calmly.

I glanced at the photo on the glass top. I could smell the sweat in the small of her back. Why would David tell them about her, except to save his own skin? She had been his idea, too. I could feel myself weaken. Then get pissed. This shit would get all around school, the whole town.

"Her dad's not too happy," the cop continued. "Says you fucked his daughter. She's thirteen years old."

"We didn't," I said.

The cop smiled. "Really? That's not what she says."

I could hear voices from the kitchen. Mom was nailing the poor guy.

Still eyes leaned in a little. "Your parents don't have to know about Judy," he said. "Just between us."

I NOTICE THE "a" in "fedora" is stuck in blood. I punch the key a couple of times. I hook the letter with my fingernail and release it, and it snaps back into place. I tap the letter; it sticks again.

The girl on the train wanted what she wanted, and I was handy, I understand that. But that's how love happens, isn't it? The minute she descended on me both of our breaths caught, and we held there for an instant, until she closed her eyes and exhaled in a soft sound of pleasure. Her hands pressed into my shoulders. She lifted up a little, and I could feel the tug of her. I glanced at her image in the window; her head was back, her throat exposed. I touched it, let my fingers slide up and down, until my thumb and forefinger closed lightly on the ridges. I pressed in a little, and then tightened the touch. Her eyes opened in a cauldron of heat. "Do it," she whispered. My hips jerked into her. She bucked, and I slammed again, grasping her rear with both hands. Fingers slid around to touch the crack, which I could feel open with the pressure. "Good," she whispered. Her hips rocked a little, massaging me. Back and forth, up and down, back and forth, up and down, until I would slam into her, pulling down on her hips at the same time, and she would hold and shudder a little, and I would stare at the whiteness of her throat reflected in the subtle starlight. I let go of watching and thinking about what I was seeing. I pushed in with my thumbs until I could feel the edge of her pubic hair. My thumbs slid down, touched the lips themselves. I spread the flesh apart, pressed onto the nub. "That's it," she said. She lifted up until I was barely inside her. There she froze, shuddered, tossed her head back, rocked once, twice, and dropped down hard onto me, with a primitive moan. Her rear was quivering in my hands. Her head fell forward. She slowly brought her eyes into focus.

She whispered, "Did we wake anyone?"

"Only the baby," I said.

ALL KEYS ARE now working, I note. And the bloodstained paper has been removed and a clean one inserted. Reading what I just wrote, I see the slenderest thread of something new, something more than sexual pleasure.

WHEN DID I decide to come here to the house on the lake? I sort back through the past several days. I dropped off Thesis—a long-haired orange male cat I'd had for five years—at a friend's house with a bag of cat food and enough money for five years' worth of medical care and food. I unhooked my telephone and tossed the answering machine down the garbage chute in the hall. The hours after that are unclear, and they're gradually becoming less and less clear, which is all right. It's not the final days I seek to understand. I admit I didn't fuck Shelley Duvall, and so what if I was cheated of the experience of having taken another's life? If the images would simply hold in pattern, march across the sky in some sort of order, to an end yet unseen but certainly there. They never have before, I chastise myself, why would you think they might now? I shake my head over the fact that I could have driven all the way up here to the little village and stood on the front porch of our vacation house and looked the caretaker in the eye before I remembered Joseph. Jesus, I could remember the color of Judy Pauling's eyes, picture the amused look on David's face when I finally confronted him about the detectives.

AFTER DROPPING OFF Thesis, I parked the old Chevy convertible in front of my second wife's apartment, with a note on the windshield, and called a cab from a corner grocery. A chattering Somali driver took me to the only car rental place in Booneville. I thought of stopping by David's print shop. It wasn't necessary, I told myself. But it would be right, I thought. Jar the story into its final reality.

In fact, I would like to see Joseph and search out the truth of what happened the long-ago afternoon of his demise. Once he'd left in the canoe, we seemed to forget all about him. Someone

would call out a game—first one across the river and back—and
then someone another game—who could dive farthest out from the
dock—until we were on the verge of fatigued hysteria. My shoulders were burned and I had a slice on the bottom of my foot, but
I wouldn't be the first one to quit. Finally, someone said, "Hey,
where's Joseph?" The sun had slid to the top of the pines, and the
air was cooling. We looked out over the lake. No sign of him. Sally
shot a glance at me, as if I were somehow complicit because I had
gone over with him a few days earlier. We walked to the edge of the
lake for a better view, searched for a shadow on the water. The life
jacket lay flat on the sand. I backed up a few feet. It struck me that
Sally might suggest that we, or at least I, jump in the second canoe
and go look for him. "He probably stayed over there, at the camp,"
I said. "I would have. Look." I pointed at a dark blotch spreading
in the middle of the lake. A good squall could dump a sizeable sail-
boat, not to mention a canoe. The others agreed. Sally stared at the
water, glanced up at the sky, now darkening, and took off in a dead
run in the direction of her family's cabin.

A READING LIGHT flicked on a few rows ahead. People rustled
about in their seats. An elderly lady wearing a dark shawl padded up the aisle to the restroom. The only sound was the relentless
clickety-clack of the steel wheels skipping over the cracks in the
steel rails, and the steady breathing of the sleeping girl, whose head
lay on my chest. Outside, the sky had deepened, although the moon
was not to be seen. Dark forms flew by like ghosts. The girl sighed
gently, as if she were in a sweet dream. Her hand rose to my neck,

and her fingers spread wide. I breathed in the strange smell of sex. I closed my eyes and allowed myself to drift with the sensations. The clinking sound of the Zippo opening brought me around. I cracked an eye: it was the elderly lady, lighting a cigarette with my lighter. She glanced at us as she puffed, and then padded on down the aisle. The peace of our little capsule was shattered by a shaft of light flashing around the inside of the car. Racing around a curve up ahead was a jittery white moon. Two whistles screamed in unison. The girl stirred. I brushed her hair back. Her eyes opened.

"Another train," I said.

Around the white eye you could barely make out a ring of black steel. The monster was aimed right at our very gut; it would lift us off the tracks and toss us over. The girl shifted in her seat, and her arms tightened around me. The white eye lit us up like ghosts. At the last moment it screeched a few degrees off, and I could feel the whoosh of the air as the black steel flashed by. Not a separation of more than ten feet, I thought. The girl sat up. The twin whistles shrieked again, and the trains rocked violently. The metal racketing vibrated the skin on my face. I placed a hand on the window. The girl placed one next to it. Boxcars flashed between our thumbs.

NOW THE SPACE key on the typewriter has stopped working. I tap it, nothing, so I tap it harder and still nothing. So, it will all run together. I hold my finger up in front of the space where the key hits and punch a key, which whacks my finger, and the carriage moves one space. It'll take too long. Still, I feel the beginning edge of a peaceful wave. I've lived long enough to get a good taste of life.

Fifty-five years, two wives, no children, a novel, a variety of lov-
ers, lots of blind alleys, vivid moments of piercing insight, walls of
sightlessness. Friends, of a sort. Students who went out of their way
to express gratitude, although fewer in the latter years, when my
emphasis shifted to the nature and origin of violence in the human
animal. I weaved relentlessly toward an inescapable determinism,
which, if followed faithfully, could only lead one to conclude that
there is no such thing as moral responsibility.

I would nod to one of the football players in the class and ask:
Suppose you were born with this need for very young girls. Would
you not curse the god who made you that way? Would you not
change yourself if you could? You wouldn't believe it was your
choice, would you? Are we not helpless in the face of our fate? As
we did not make ourselves, so we cannot change ourselves. All else
is delusion. The discomfort on the students' faces usually began to
show by the second class.

"So what would you do with the guy who rapes little girls?" a
student asked in frustration.

"What would you do?" I responded.

"Give him the death penalty. Kill him."

"To make yourself feel better."

"To stop him from doing it again."

"Life in prison would do that."

"He deserved it."

"But his death would make you feel better, wouldn't it?"

I could never understand their reluctance to admit the obvious.
It's why we do everything we do.

"Uh-huh."

And on it went. Several of the girls and one or two boys dropped the class. Others added when the word got out. I experimented with different methods of making what I thought was a fairly simple and obvious point: nothing transcends nature, nothing exists outside it, or is separate from it. I would pose a hypothetical. Imagine, I told a student, that you have a six-year-old daughter. One night you are awakened to a noise; you search the house and find her missing from her bedroom. You grab a knife from the kitchen. You find a man holding her on the floor in the garage behind your house. The man has her knees apart and is bending over her.

I kept the story going in vivid detail, until finally the student jumped to his feet, raised the knife overhead, and lunged at the figure on the floor. With a cry, he brought the blade down into the man's back. Several women began weeping. Others looked away or walked out. I later asked those who remained to write up their version of the incident and their reaction to it. No one felt anything for the man; no one, despite my imprecations, saw him simply as the product of a careless or ill-intentioned creator. Suppose it was a python who had wrapped itself around the girl as she slept in her crib and squeezed the life from her? I asked. Would you blame the python? Would you fall into a fit of rage and stab it full of holes? No? Why not? Nature, they'd reply, as if man himself were somehow unnatural.

THE SENTENCES ARE beginning to have a frantic feel to them, as if they might tumble off the end of the paper. I raise the cover

and poke around inside, until I find a little rod that seems to have
slipped out of its hole. I manage to force it back in. Tap, tap. The
space key works. My fingers are covered with ink. I wipe them on
my pants and see what looks like a red stain just above the knee
on the right leg. I poke at it with a thumb; it's dry, but not crusty.
I press in and feel a sharp pain. I sort back through the day. Not
surprisingly, my narrative is sparse and uneven. The gaps are spaces
with no hints around the edges. The cat. The car. A hot midday sun
with a thread of cool air in it. My briefcase on the kitchen table.
An open newspaper next to it. On the kitchen counter I see a sharp
wide blade attached to a black handle with two rivets in it, sticking
point-up from the utensil box on the dish rack. I squint in my mind,
trying to collect the pieces, sort out the puzzle. I had awoken this
morning to a cool autumn sun. I was writing an article for *Human
Nature* magazine on the wellspring of human motivation, but I had
lingered beyond the submission date and had found within myself
little desire to bend back into it. It seemed like a woman had crept
from the bed in the first edge of dawn and slipped into her clothes
and out of the room. But whom? The sun was midway up the east
window by the time I swung out of bed. The slanting rays lit the
living room on fire, yet the wood floors were still cold. Draft pages
of my article were scattered on the living room floor as if flung
about by a child. Two chairs were pulled out at the round breakfast
room table by the front window. At each place was an empty wine
glass. Then the briefcase, and the newspaper, laying half open. It
didn't add up. I didn't feel a woman on my skin. Taste her. I picked
up a wine glass, spotted a coral smudge on the rim. Of course.

She always wore the same color. I could hear the door close, the high heels clacking down the wooden stairs. I walked into the small kitchen and set the glasses in the pocked porcelain sink. Thesis brushed through my legs. Sun-fire caught the blade of the knife. It was incredibly beautiful. I flicked a finger down the edge.

The flow of images is, as always, somewhat suspect. I remember feeding Thesis from a half-empty tin of tuna in the fridge, then stepping to the window. The scene outside was very bright, almost painfully so, and the street seemed quite distant, as if of another world. A woman in a station wagon pulled into a spot in front of the small grocery next to the café and got out. I looked more closely. I recognized the thick chestnut hair pulled back and woven into a single braid, the gentle sway in her thin body as she stepped on the curb. Years ago her son had taken my Philosophy of Violence class. She had come to my office to talk about his reaction to the content. She was more curious than upset. Had I been subject to violence as a child? Did I believe violence was a natural state or behavior? My answers must have turned her on, for we ended up having sex on my desk. Her sweaty bottom printed on the proof of an article I was editing. The next year the school installed window air conditioners.

Now I think I might have been mixing up the sex part with another woman, a colleague. It really doesn't make any difference, does it? It got me where I am, which is not a particularly bad place, and if you rework it, if you rework any story, you could end up somewhere else. Which is how I got here, in this tiny moonlit room, with inky fingers and what appears to be a bloodstained tear on my jeans. Because I reworked the story a little.

I remember turning from the kitchen window as the burbling of the percolator on the counter behind me reached a fever pitch. I didn't drink coffee, but I liked the sound of it perking and the smell of it, which wafted through my small place like an almond perfume. Bright and shiny, with a glass top, the percolator was a wedding gift from the first marriage. My wife and I were driving home from a party when she told me she was leaving. It was two years after I had caught her fucking David. She was leaving to be with him.

I grabbed the small brass handle on the kitchen window and jerked it up. A curtain blew in my face. I pushed it away, felt an autumn sting on my face, and stared through watery eyes at the door to the small grocery. It swung open, and the woman walked out, arms full of sacks. She lifted the rear gate on the station wagon and bent in a little as she set the sacks down. I leaned out and watched as she opened the driver's door, got in, and looked over her shoulder to back up. I raised a hand. She caught it, and our eyes held for an instant. She smiled faintly and cranked the wheel. It's not her, I thought as she backed out and pulled away. Just like it wasn't the girl on the train in the main hall on campus years earlier. Just like there are no strange noises in this old house.

I picked up the wine glasses and examined them for a hint of coral on the rim. Nothing. Thesis jumped up on the counter and sniffed them, as if to help out. I lifted him to the floor. The answer lay in the other room, on the table. I glanced at the glowing tip of the knife as I passed by. The living room was awash in dust motes. The brass clasp on the battered leather briefcase sitting on the white plastic cloth shone like a gold star. Next to it was a square glass ashtray with a half-smoked butt in the crevice. Next to that was the *Booneville County Register.* The front section was open. I walked a step or two into the room. Turn around, I thought, go out the door. I stepped closer. A headline at the top of the page stated: "Man Found Dead in Alley." Beneath it was an image of an elderly man, probably in his mid-eighties, with wisps of hair across his pate and thin, almost invisible lips. It was him: Willie Benson, the man who had promised to get us girls. The same sharp eyes. His name was written beneath the photo; the lines read that an elderly Booneville man had been found dead in an alley between First and Main. A paramedic reported that his throat appeared to have been slit and that he had stab wounds in the back of the neck. The article read that Benson was eighty-six and had a criminal record, but didn't say what it was. Police had no leads. And didn't give a fuck, I thought. No one gives a fuck. Which is too bad. Willie was who he was. Certainly, were it up to him, he would have chosen a different configuration of needs and desires. You didn't have to forgive Willie, or even sympathize with him; you just had to understand his origin, to place him along the continuum of nature, in which there is no murder, in which there are no unnatural acts.

The steel radiator on the far wall of the living room began clanging. In my single room at prep school, the radiators had hissed and banged away half the night in the winter months. It wasn't that cold in my apartment, but suddenly, every radiator in the place was clanging, a terrible, punishing three-note orchestra. I clapped my hands over my ears. I yelled at them to stop. They clanged happily on until my skull bones were vibrating. I sank to my knees, touched my forehead to the floor. The clanging slowly lessened, grew fainter. The steam vents whistled, first the one in the living room, then the ones in the bedroom and the bathroom. All together they shrieked. I rolled over on my back and wiped the tears from my eyes. So now he's dead. After all these years, someone finally stuck him. The sound of laughter from my throat relaxed me.

I GLANCE OVER at the briefcase on the floor. Inside, I suspect, is the rest of the newspaper. Perhaps other things. I press my thumb hard into the tear in my jeans. Even with that, the images refuse to loosen up and roll. I see Thesis lying on my stomach, looking at me with interest. I want to scratch his head, but my arms are stuck to the floor. That's where the show ends. I flick off the lamp. The moon has grown so large and bright the room is aglow.

When did I know the true story of Willie and David and me? Do I know it now? It floats loose in the liquid of my brain, never clear and sharp, never hooked up, never logical, never appearing when you think. Looking back, it—the story—is a feeling wrapped in gauze. The girl with the alluring pain-struck eyes had sensed it. It was why she wanted me. A communion of damaged souls, I see now. Even if it wasn't my idea; even if I hadn't participated in anything, I had been there, I had watched it, and said nothing. It had clung unseen to me every day since, like the smell from the meatpacking plants on the edge of town.

ON THE TRAIN, I dozed while the girl dreamed. When I came around, I had a thirst and a scratchy feeling inside my skull. Her head on my chest felt like a smooth stone. My hands had freed themselves of her. I could be anyone in this seat. Any boy. Nothing by morning. I was lost in her flesh. Lost to myself. Uneasy, uncertain, uncomfortable, unsafe, I wanted free of it, of her, to be sitting across the aisle, forgotten, put back together, empty-headed except for patterns of translucent stars whirling about in the formless heavens. I touched her head.

"I need to get a drink," I whispered.

Her eyes opened.

"Sorry," I said. She murmured something, lifted her head. Her hair was tousled; her lips unpainted. I avoided her eyes. It all seemed kind of tawdry, after the fact. Like we should both wash up.

"Hey," she said. "Don't go."

"I've got to pee." I looked at her, hoping for release, but instead saw disappointment. She withdrew her hand, and I stood and stepped shakily into the aisle. I made my way forward, touching the seats to steady myself, seeing everything as if it were a sharply different reality. My legs felt weak, my breathing faint. It should be better than this, I thought. Your first blow job, your first piece of ass. You should be flying in glory.

I opened a door to a small, dimly lit vestibule. Along one wall was a fabric-covered bench. Across the space was a small, shiny metal sink, and over that a long mirror with a light above it. A narrow door led to the toilet itself. The room smelled of Pine-Sol. Lights flashed in the window as the train began to slow. The train jerked to a stop. I pressed my face against the window, encircled it with my hands. The light on a tall pole illuminated

a small brick building with a sign on it, which read in black letters: "Smithville." Two men in wool caps and heavy jackets were
throwing bags of mail from a boxcar onto a two-wheeled wooden
cart. One of the men waved and shouted something and the train
jerked back hard. My shoulder banged into the window frame.
As we began creeping up the track, I saw the men pushing the
mail cart into a doorway at the side of the station. We passed an
unpaved street with a few lights and a café and bank, and after
that rows of small wood frame houses, each one as dark as the
other. The spindly, ghostly shape of a water tower loomed up
behind them, and then Smithville was gone and we were slicing
through rolling fields of grain.

I stepped into a room so tiny I couldn't straighten up. I steadied
myself in front of the metal toilet and unzipped my pants. I worked
my dick out. For all the pounding and throbbing and excitement
not too long ago, it now seemed a small, harmless thing. I shook
it a few times, to bring it around, and then remembered I really
didn't have to pee. I concentrated, and when a weak stream finally
began I reached out with my other hand and twisted the handle on
the wall. The metal flap snapped open, and down the chute I could
see racing blurs of rocks and wooden ties. The clickety-clack was
suddenly a tremendous clatter of machine guns, and the whoosh of
air sucked the pee out in a mist. The metal racking grew louder and
harder, until thinking became impossible. I stood at an angle over
the toilet and allowed the shattering noise to flow through my legs
and chest and up into my cheek and jaw bones, until I was rattling
right along with it in perfect balance. My hand dropped from the

handle, and the flap snapped shut. I was left in a deafening silence, and I fell back against the wall.

MY EYES OPEN slowly. I've been nodding off. A sliver of panic rushes my throat; how long was I gone? How much time have I left? This drifting away in the middle of scenes is unfortunate. Time runs in a straight line, and the end of the line is the end of the line. The images splice and separate and hook up and fly away and crumble and linger in large and small forms; like right now, the Zippo is shining crisply in the light of the moon. On one side is the Marine Corps emblem; I remember how I used to rub it with my thumb and think of the boys who died on the sands and rocks of Iwo Jima. "Hard rain gonna fall," Leon Russell used to sing. Toward the end of her life, my mother told me what my father was like before the war on that island broke him. Tough, smart, ambitious—a leader. The Zippo? He had brought it home, along with a carbine, a .45 sidearm, and a Jap helmet. (I can feel the top of the lighter snap open, hear the unmistakable clink, which is different from the clunk when you snap it shut. I can hear them one after the other. Clink. Clunk.) My father never spoke of the war or what happened on that island, but I heard the story from a friend of his who was there. My father's squad was out of ammunition, and they were getting heavy fire from a company of Japs on a ridge about two hundred yards away. Two of his men were shredded by a wave of machine gun fire. My father rose from his foxhole with a bayonet on the end of his rifle and charged screaming up the hill. He gutted one Jap, and then another, and covered in blood he charged straight into the machine gun nest and stabbed two more in the chest, taking one bullet in his thigh and another in his shoulder. Afterward, when the Japs had pulled back, he returned to the enemy lying on the ground and stuck them one by one through the heart. When he got back to Booneville two years later, he veered away from a planned career in the law and ran a hardware store on the main street of town until he died of a heart attack at age forty-nine.

I am caught by the orange glow of the moon. I stand and walk around the table to the window. The stars seem to have fallen away from it, leaving it in a dark hole. Half the night left, at most. A couple of hours. Nothing in this story will stand the light of day. The strip of light in the water is wider and softer and tinged orange as well. Joseph had floated into shore that night, whether in the moonlight or not I don't know. Washed up in branches, face up, eyes open, he would have stared into eternity.

I tilt to the left, to accommodate the jerk of the train to the right. I see the boy in the vestibule sitting on the bench and laying his head back. Trying to calm the swirling images in his head. He knows but he doesn't know; he sees but he doesn't see. He doesn't want to leave, go back down the aisle to his seat, the girl. He's best alone now.

I SNAPPED THE door to the repair shop behind me. It was the day after the detectives' visit, and I had come to confront David about why he had ratted me out. He was talking to the postman, who was taking a lawn mower engine apart on the bench. When he saw my face, David stopped talking. He tilted his head and walked out the back door. I followed him. The screen door slapped shut behind me.

"The cops came to my house," I said.

He pulled a pack of sunflower seeds from his jean jacket and stuck a handful in his mouth. He began cracking the shells and spitting them onto the small cement apron, already stained with butts and spittle.

"Yeah, mine, too," he said.

"Why'd you give them my name?"

"They already had it," he said.

"It was your fucking wallett," I said. "They showed it to me, along with your picture of Judy Pauling."

"It's no big deal," he said. "Willie's in jail."

Yeah, he is. Your friend. You set it up. It was your idea. So I said it: "It was your goddamn idea."

"Take it easy," he said. "Have a weed." He pulled a pack of tall Pall Malls from his shirt pocket, shook it, held it out. I grabbed it out of reflex. I was supposed to take it easy? David struck a match. The weed stayed at my side.

"Hey," he said. "I talked to Judy this morning. She's up for a party."

"She told the cops we fucked her," I said.

He chuckled. "The cops made that up. I was with her last night. She asked about you. And," he said, "it was your wallett, not mine."

"Bullshit," I burst out. "I saw the fucking thing. It was yours."

He shook out the match, dropped it on the cement.

"It was your fucking idea," I insisted.

"It was your wallett," he responded. "How do you think the cops got to you? They talked to you first."

THE BOY SEATED on the bench in the vestibule on the train doesn't know any of this; or if he knows it, it's not connected with any filament leading to his consciousness. Same here: I couldn't have told you about the sunflower seeds or the Pall Mall or Judy Pauling. The wallett? Not that either; nor that he claimed the one the cops had was mine. My narrative ran the way I've described: I went along with it because it was his idea. The detective with the dead eyes, or the one with the river on his cheek; neither of them said the thing was mine. They didn't say either way, as best I can remember. As a matter of fact, I still don't believe it was mine. It was David's idea, it was his friend, and it was his wallett. And everything else that happened that afternoon was his doing.

I could hear the sputtering of a lawn mower engine in the shop behind me. My green-and-white Schwinn, with my baseball glove hanging on a handlebar, was leaning against a pole in front of the shop. I was ready to head out for a game of pickup in the lot behind the junior high.

A queasiness holds me in place. You went along on your own accord. No one forced you. You agreed. You walked through the sour smell of stale food down the hall to the last room on the left.

My belief that telling the story of the night on the train, the night with the girl, would somehow bring me closer to the truth, while irrational on its face, seems to be playing out. One of the reasons

I had only written a novel about a murder and denied myself the experience of it was the belief that the crime would ruin the rest of my days. The joy of killing would be smothered in remorse and guilt. This ability to predict what I was going to feel after the act, whatever it was, was primarily a curse. It didn't necessarily stop me—like stealing dollar bills from my father's wallett on his dresser while he sat in his robe at the breakfast table—but it prepared me. So the boy knew from instinct what it would be like taking the truth of that afternoon with him through the rest of his days. He didn't *know* it; he understood it the way he understood that he was left-handed. If I could modify my design, I would delete this predictive ability. In fact, I would delete the wiring for shame and remorse altogether. Not to mention guilt.

I jab my thumb into the wound on my thigh, and a bolt of pain brings me to life.

I SAT ON the bench in the vestibule in a soft stupor. I'd been on the road for over a day by then and had close to another one to go. The girl already seemed to be turning into a memory. A shadow fell over me. I opened my eyes. It was her. Her hair was pulled back into a ponytail.

"There you are," she said.

Her hands were on her hips.

"I got really tired," I said, slumping even further.

"Poor baby," she said, turning back and throwing the bolt on the door. Her skirt, I noticed, fell just above the knee.

"Do you know where we are?" I asked.

"Right here," she said, "you and me."

Not me, I thought. I'm gone. The heat and the wet and the stiff-ness and the sounds and smells—it was over. None of it seemed to bother her. She flicked off the overhead light, and in the reach for the switch her skirt pulled up a little, emphasizing the gentle rise of her bottom. I looked away, out the window. We were racing over the plains now, the no-man's-land of corn and wheat fields long since shorn of their produce. A blackness speckled by lights here and there, but no cars, no moon in sight.

I felt the seat depress next to me. The girl placed a hand on my neck and kissed my forehead.

I looked at her, felt the depths of her eyes.

"I'm shot," I said.

Her face sweetened. "I understand."

She stood and walked two steps across the tiny room to the sink. She flicked on a light over the mirror and looked at herself. She loosened her ponytail, ran her hands through her hair, and fluffed it out. Her eyes dropped a fraction, to look at me. I sat up. Tiny white lights flashed on the periphery of my vision. She pulled her blouse down and tucked it in, never taking her eyes off me. She adjusted her cupcake-like tits under the sweater. The white dots began flashing. I could feel the blood pulse through my fingers. As if sensing it, she dropped her eyes, and I sucked in a deep breath. The barest of smiles hinted at her lips. Retrieving a gold tube from a small purse at her side, she glanced at her mouth in the mirror. She twisted the tube until a red stick appeared. She leaned over slightly, and the back of her skirt rose an inch. She opened her mouth and tugged at her upper lip with the stick, then rubbed her lips together. She leaned in a fraction more, which caused her bottom to push out and the center of her skirt—and I assumed her bottom—to separate a little. She gave me a look. The upper lip was red as a cherry. My lungs seemed to have stopped inflating. She leaned a little further forward, and her skirt rose nearly to the top of her thigh. The train lurched to the right and she caught a handrail and took a small step. The tiny lights were exploding in color.

Her hand dropped to her side. In scrawled red letters on the glass was written:

NOW

I TAKE A deep breath, snap my eyes shut, and lean back in the chair. Her hand is holding the golden tube by her side. The red stick has disappeared. Her eyes hold no challenge, only invitation. Over the years, the scene often stops at that very moment. I dwell on the possibilities of it, rather than the realities. But tonight, I want it to continue on, through the heat and the explosion, to the other side, where we've returned to the seats and are in each other's arms. I want to listen for any words between us. Hear the screeching of the wheels and feel the jolts of the train as we pull into the Chicago station. See the colors changing in her mysterious eyes in the gray light of morning.

I FEEL A slight chill. My coat is flung on the chair, next to the briefcase. An Irish tweed I wore for the last ten years teaching in the classroom. Jeans and black-and-white Keds, with paper-thin

soles, like I wore as a boy when I wasn't in my cowboy boots.
Not the same shoes, of course, although I still had my original Roy
Rogers twin pistol set hanging from a hook in the living room of
my small apartment. The leather holster is edged in brightly colored glass beads. I used to stand in front of the full-length mirror
in my parents' bedroom and practice a cross draw, staring straight
into my own eyes, waiting for someone to flinch. I wore the holster and a felt cowboy hat and boots to cowboy movies downtown
on Saturday morning. That was well before Willie. Before Joseph.
Before the girl on the train.

My second wife used to say that there was really never a place
for me in this world, that I was always half in it and half out of it.
My exploration of a philosophy of violence intrigued and scared
her. She was tempted, as were many women, to see it as a moral
release to commit mayhem without consequence.

I lean down and tie both laces. I am lightheaded when I
straighten up. I brush the goose bumps on my arms and think of
putting on my jacket. I can't quite track my movements from the
moment I saw Willie's picture in the paper until I picked up the
rental car and drove out of town. A particularly violent way to kill
an old man, I remember thinking. What was he doing in an alley
in the first place? I see the alley now, clear and crisp, with shadows
and sounds, and I see where Willie lay dying. A dark red stain a few
feet from a row of battered trash cans. A feral black cat licking the
edge of it. Willie, Willie, I think. A life as real as any other, played
out from cradle to grave, ending on cold cement. Not an unfitting
end, really, but one can seek balance in existence, yin for yang,

good for bad, without giving into an emotional storm about it. The killer's arm must have surged as he jerked the knife up in Willie's throat, filleting it like a fish. Violence based in hate or anger is never clean; it leaves a poison behind.

A DARK CLOUD spins in the middle of the lake. It quickly thickens. The oak leaves dance. The cloud blackens further and rises until it begins blotting out the light of the moon, like an eclipse. Rain spatters against the window, the moon disappears. I step up and touch the panes and feel the vibrations in my finger bones. Squalls, I remember, usually arise in the afternoons, not at night. They come and they go, sometimes in a matter of minutes, often with vicious force. You don't fight it; you give into it; you wait it out. If it flips your boat, you stay with the craft. You resist panic. The night is so black now I can see nothing. As if I'm blind. Water slaps the window. I can feel the life jacket tight under my arms, pushing roughly up into my chin. My arms are churning helplessly. My head is smacked by a wall of water. I cough and gasp for breath, sucking in more water. My glasses are gone, but through the black winds I can make out the shape of the canoe, upside down, twisting in the wind-churned water. Hanging onto the end of it is a shadowy form. Joseph. He's screaming my name. I pull toward the canoe. We're not that far from the shore, I think. I tug the top strap on the vest a little tighter. Thank God for it. My limbs are chilling. My eyes sting. I hear my name again, fainter this time. I turn over on my back and stroke in the direction of the sound. The canoe suddenly looms on a wave a few yards in front of me. I see Joseph with one hand locked onto the edge of the craft.

"Joseph!" I call out, but the words wash back in my face. A wave pushes me closer, and through a break in the black wind I can see him. His eyes are wild, one arm is flailing.

"Stay with the canoe," I yell. Always stay with the canoe. My arms pull in his direction. I feel them tiring as the chill hits the bone. I kick. Something is wrong, I think. I hesitate. What is it? I manage a few feet closer to him. I can see the panic in his eyes now. He's wearing himself out. "Take it easy," I shout.

He sees me and flails more fiercely. I can see a white T-shirt. No vest. No need, he had said. I had tossed an extra one under my seat, but it was long gone by now.

I can't see at all now. Either my eyes are shut, the squall has blotted out the sky, or I've gone blind. I lift the latch on the window and push it open. The wind jerks the window from my hand, bangs it against the side of the house. Water lashes my face. Now I'm out in it. There is no canoe. There is no moon. I can see nothing. It's a good story. If I hadn't looked into the caretaker's eyes, I would still be seeing and writing about the girl on the train. No struggling boy in the water screaming my name. I open my eyes and squint: nothing, not even the oak branches, which I can hear twisting and slapping the house. The vest tightens on me. I push my chest out and hold it there. Joseph's features are contorted in fear. The squall is pushing him toward me. A few feet away he begins to drop until only his chin is poking out of the water. A hand grasps for me. I reach for it.

I STEP BACK, from the window. I glance around into pure darkness. Images like those of Joseph and me in the squall are not what I would call trustworthy, certainly not a literal recitation of an event, but neither can they be dismissed simply as the products of an unstable mind. As old narratives fall away, new ones take their place. Nature abhors a vacuum, as they say. That I have no memory of paddling over to the camp, or talking to any girls, means nothing. The look on Joseph's face as he reaches for me—I can't see making that one up. But nothing of the event for all these years, nearly a lifetime? I wouldn't say I forgot about the detectives at the door, or even Willie, for that matter; it nibbled at the edges, never in story form, and I would say, standing here, apparently blind, for the moment, that I'm still not clear as to what actually happened that afternoon, except that it wasn't my wallett on the floor.

I raise my arms. I step sideways until my hand brushes the wall. I stare in the direction of the window. Willie's room was damp and musty. David sat in one chair and I in the other. Willie sat on the edge of the bed. The window was open to the sounds of children on the sidewalk. Finally, I said: "Where's the girl?"

THANK GOD FOR the night on the train. Finally aroused, I rose from the bench and stood behind her. I felt her bottom. I paused at the heat of it, even through the skirt. My hand slipped under the material, my finger pushed in, and she gasped, and another finger pushed in. Her bottom pressed back into my hand. I glanced in the mirror: her eyes were shut. With my other hand I lifted up her skirt. The flesh was white as alabaster. I stared at where my fingers disappeared. I moved them in and out, once, twice, then pushed them in hard and watched the white flesh jiggle. She tossed her head back until I could see the ripples in her throat.

There was a loud rapping on the door. We froze in place. How were we going to explain this?

"WHAT'S GOING ON in there?" a woman's voice called. "I have to use the toilet."

The door knob jiggled. I pulled her skirt down, but left my hand where it was.

"I'm sick," the girl called out toward the door.

Pause.

"There's two of you," the voice muttered.

The girl smiled wickedly at me in the mirror. "Just a friend," she said.

A snort sounded from the other side of the door.

"Next car," I said in a hoarse voice. "Just through the doors."

Pause. A final twist of the knob. The car doors hissed open.

"She's gone," I whispered.

IN THE DARKNESS I hear Joseph's voice, calling my name. I consider searching for a light switch I remember seeing on the wall by the door. The light in the lamp was on, and yet now there is only darkness. I turn toward the chair; no visible briefcase, no jacket. I stamp the floor. I hold my arms in front of me. The window bangs against the house. Water whips across my face. Joseph's voice is in my head, not out there. This blackness is in my head, as well. The girl on the train is in my head. Was I even on the train? I grasp the wood trim of the oval window. That's real. Willie was real. I can smell his cheap aftershave. Willie was an Aqua Velva man. "Where is the girl?" I ask. I see the red splotch on the cold cement alley. The cat's paws are brightly stained. There never was a girl; there was never supposed to be a girl. From the beginning I knew it. Someone should have hosed the blood down. I take a step toward the splotch. It is crusting around the edges, but there is a bright crimson gash in the middle.

I'm getting chilled. I rub my arms. Suddenly, the pressure seems to drop. The squall winds begin weakening. On top of the blackness is a golden shimmer. The moon is shining down on the storm. Bands of stars appear. I lean out the window and reach for the oval frame. I grab it, and for a moment hang there in the balance. Below me is the garden and the lake-stone wall and the sharp cliff and, barely visible, the inky water below. The blackness of the squall evaporates. An eerie silence takes its place. A dark form seemed to be working its way to shore, sliding in on top of the waves.

I lean an inch further and pull hard; the window gives way so suddenly that I lose my balance and almost tumble backward.

I couldn't say how long the detectives stayed that morning, so many years ago, but now it's so fresh in my mind that I can feel the smoke fill my lungs as I drag on the fancy weed and sense but not see the terrible judgment in my mother's eyes. My father had returned but was sitting on a chair across the room, waiting for it to be over. A lawn mower started up outside, and I tracked its sound as it grew closer and then moved on. The second detective leaned in and said: "David told us what happened. You didn't do anything wrong. We just need to hear it from you." Suddenly, I got it: David had lied to them. Told them I was involved. It fit him; he always saw things the way that suited him best, and in this case that meant pointing the finger at me. My neck grew hot. Through the front window I could see a neighbor's car slow as it passed the detectives' vehicle. The detective lay a photo of Willie on the glass table. "You know him," he said. The lawn mower grew louder, as if it had moved into our yard. It was David, not me, I almost said. His idea. He tapped David's photo without taking his eyes off me. That's right, him. The two of them. Him and Willie. I felt myself nod, and words formed in my mind. If they wanted to know what happened, I would tell them what happened. Starting with the wallett.

"Tell them," my mother said. I looked up. The revulsion in her eyes was really saying the opposite. She understood that whatever I had done would only get worse if I admitted it. (Not that she ever doubted that I had done it.) The detectives got her message, too. The heavyset one with the river scar spoke: "We'll be filing a report with the juvenile probation department."

"We just want to get Willie off the street," the first detective said, "put him in jail where he belongs."

They needed a witness, someone to take the stand and testify as to what happened. Both of us needed to tell the same story. They didn't care who had done what, as long as it matched up. My mother must have seen it, too. It would get out, around town, before the sun set on the day.

"My son doesn't lie."

The detective broke a cynical grin. "He's already lied."

It was over. You didn't challenge my mother. The second detective sensed it, tried to pull it out. He put his note pad away and sat back in his chair. I could have told him it was no use. It was over for them. I finally had a protector. "We can handle this quietly," he said. "It won't go to court. Willie's been in jail before; he knows how it works." The lawn mower suddenly quit, and the room fell silent. My mother seemed to look at both of them at once. They were now intruders on her turf. And they knew it. The river scar sighed. My mother walked in the direction of the door. He picked up the two photos and stuck them back in the wallett. He folded it shut, held it out, and started to say something.

"Call first next time," my mother said. She pulled the door open. The detectives rose in unison, my father stood up.

THE AIR IN the room was heavy. The window was open a foot, but the gauzy white curtains hung straight and still. In a cheap gold frame over the bed was a picture of Jesus with a radiating heart in his chest. A brown nubby spread covered the small bed. No girl. There wasn't even a bathroom in the place. Willie shut the door and snapped the lock. Have a seat, he said, pointing to the single wood chair against the wall. David motioned for me to sit, but I stayed where I was. Willie sat on the edge of the bed. His pale forehead was shiny.

"Where's the girl?" I asked again.

"She got held up," he said. "She'll be here soon."

David didn't seem surprised by this. A look passed between them.

"She's a piece of ass," David said. "Red hair, up and down." He twirled his hands in front of him, meaning big tits.

I wanted badly to believe him.

"Tight pussy."

"You fucked her?" This wasn't part of the story he'd been telling.

"Just felt it," he said, grinning.

I would have heard of this earlier if it had happened. The whole thing was a story. Willie's small, dark eyes darted between us.

"She'll suck your dick," he said.

David looked out the window, as if she might be coming up the walk at this very moment. The curtains jumped in a puff of air. I could feel the heat.

"There needs to be something in this for me," Willie said.

THE CLICKING OF the typewriter keys reverberates in my head, as if to remind me of steel wheels spinning over steel rails and to get on with the story of the night on the train. I twist the knob and slip the paper out, stick a new one in behind the roller, and twist the knob again. I lay the page on top of the bloodstained one. Let it go, I thought. There is nothing to fear now, and maybe there never was. Joseph is long dead; you owe his father and Sally nothing. Willie is dead, too. I glance at my briefcase, wherein still lies the article. Let the thin thread snap. I suck in a deep breath, let my chest collapse. The squall has passed. The blue-black sky and

yellow moon fill the window. David, I realize, is a blank. I can't
pull him into my mind. I pick up the top page from the stack. As I
feared, it is stuck to the one beneath it. I shake it, and it separates.
On the back of the page is a vague imprint of blood. I study it for
meaning, like a Rorschach card.

THE RESTROOM SCENE in the train is fading. Losing its color, its
vitality. The boy seems to be barely there. He watches the girl rear-
range her sweater. He wants to want her, but he feels no force in
his body. Her glance in the mirror catches him, and he looks away.
Now you see what you have, he thinks. You've wasted your night.
He looks over at the door.

The scene is stuck there. With him in collapse. Her looking at
him in the mirror, with eyes now soft and concerned. I squeeze my
eyes shut, let them drift open. I tap on the space bar several times.
Listen intently for sounds. The scene is now like an ink etching,
bereft of color and texture. It can't end like this, I think. It will
leave us all nowhere. It's not too much to ask, I insist. A little peace
at the end. I know better than to force it, but Jesus, the boy came
so far. I look away from the scene, into the blackness beyond the
moon and stars. What difference does it make? You owe him clarity, I answer. He doesn't understand. It all swirls in his soul. The
wallett. The life jacket. Even what is yet to come. You mustn't feel
sorry for him. The girl understands. I would shake him if I could.
I try to imagine another scene, to distract my mind. I see the cold
light of a winter morning as we pull into the Chicago train yards.
Everything is bright but unmoving, frozen in black and white, like

a scene on an old postcard. "Chicago," the rough voice calls out. "End of the line."

The concern in the girl's eyes lingers, but she sees the boy's features have come back to life. She sees a tenderness she had missed before.

MY FINGERS RISE from the keys and brush my neck, nick a rough edge I hadn't noticed before. The tear in my thigh pulses. I'd forgotten about it. I grab hold of the edge of the torn jean and rip it back to reveal a three-inch-long gash. I pull the lamp over to the edge of the desk, bend it low over my wound. The edges of the gash are crusted, but a bright red is seeping out the center. I rip the jean back until my thigh is exposed to the knee, and there I spot it: the old scar a few inches below the new one. I hadn't gone to the doctor for several days after ripping it on the fence in Judy Pauling's backyard. I told my mother I had fallen off my bike. The doctor, who worked out of a house at the end of our street, said it was almost too late to close, but threaded a few stitches in anyway. I had bragged about it afterward, my battle scar, a wound suffered in the unsuccessful pursuit of pussy. Over the years the scar had shrunk some, but now it seemed to glisten fiercely in the light. The new one was ragged, and deeper, cut voraciously. I pressed in on it; pinkish blood spurted from the crust. I felt the pulse again, but this time there was no pain.

I recall that the main character in my novel *The Professor* went about his murderous deed without concern or care. Some said he must have had a cold heart. I agree: Cold enough that he knew neither remorse nor guilt would follow in the path of his deeds. He was a free actor, in other words. He could move through the world without fear of consequences, because in his makeup there was no place for them to land. I think we secretly envy him his ability to live his life in neutral, our natural state of being.

I'M OFF THE track. Night will soon fail. I read through some early pages of the train ride to move back into the story. The boy's reaction to the girl and his first true sexual experience of any note seem strangely muted, as if he's watching it all from a distance, and he can't quite decide how far in he wants to go; or better, how much of it, of her, he can handle. He's in, he's out, he wants more, he wants less, he wants to hold her forever, he wants to be alone in his seat. Maybe it's simply the matter-of-fact way I'm writing the scene. Maybe something is lost in the translation into words. The girl is trying to free him, you can tell. She sees his incompleteness and wants to bring him more alive, and she believes in this one lonely night on the rails she can do something for him. The boy didn't see it that way. He felt the distance, but it seemed natural to him, and he satisfied himself with the physical sensations of sex. He memorized the experience as it was happening, perhaps in fear that it will be lost to him if he doesn't burn it into his brain. Wake up! I want to shout at him. But of course it's me writing it, so I would be screaming at myself. It's my version of how that night went that is the account of it; the boy, were he available, might tell it much differently. The years since have colored it. Truth is nowhere to be found, but that's nothing new. Glimpses here and there, through

thin clouds of dust. He was happy that night. And not just because
the girl fucked him. The flat tone is in my writing, and there's little
to be done about it, and now that I understand it, I don't care. In
fact, I'm pulling for the girl, because I don't quite remember how
the rest of the story goes. She is determined, along with everything
else, for reasons beyond me, then or now, to lead the boy out of
the haze.

What if I had told her about Willie? About Joseph? David?
Perhaps she would have loved me for my courage. Maybe we would
have stayed together. Maybe I wouldn't be here now. A love that
never faded. But what would I have told her? The boy's memories,
at least the way I recall, were very vague and not subject to a linear
recitation. Not unlike now, really. The past lay like a terrible storm
beyond the horizon: something in you is always waiting for it to
blow in, but it never hits. There was a moment in the restroom on
the train when it seemed like it might. The girl's face in the mirror
was gentle and receptive. The relentless click-clacking of the wheels
had faded into silence. But I could not find a word to begin with. I
looked away, and then back. She was a stranger.

I see now that my fear had transformed her. But in the moment
all I could feel was loneliness turning into a raging lust. I didn't
want to just fuck her, I wanted to punish her. I placed one hand
on her neck to hold her in place, and with the other I pulled my
dick from my pants. I lifted up her skirt, and ran my cock down
the crack until I felt wetness. I sought resistance on her face, maybe
even a little fear, but her eyes were closed.

"OK," I said.

I lurched forward and jammed into her. I grabbed both shoulders, pulled back and pushed in deeper, hearing a guttural sound from my throat. Her head dropped. I grabbed a handful of hair and jerked her head back. She cried out, and I jerked it back further, until her white throat was arched and her mouth was forced open. I heard the slapping of flesh on flesh.

The girl was waiting.

"Fuck you," she said.

I grasped her hips with both hands and bucked into her hard. Her head banged into the mirror.

The lights dimmed. Flickered, went off. The room was dark, except for lights flashing by in the window.

"See what you did?" she said.

I laughed, she laughed, and then we both were laughing, exhausted. The lights came back on, flickered, then stayed. I glanced at her in the mirror. Her eyes held mine. On her forehead was a red streak. And a crimson smear on the mirror. I started to back away. "No!" she cried and pushed back into me. Her hands reached back around and grabbed my hips.

BLOOD EVERYWHERE. ON her forehead, my nose, beading around Shelley's neck, on the very page, my first wife's wedding dress, my thigh, the cat's whiskers, the white face of the moon, and the pavement where Willie had lain. My hand, the palm. Was that Willie's blood I had tasted? I glance at the briefcase a few feet away: The blotch on the handle his as well? Here, in my lost city of refuge? What had I done? I needed the truth of this day, as well

as what had come before, I was coming to see, and I knew that if
you sought the truth you couldn't open the door a few inches, let a
crack of light in, and then shut it.

The Professor grasped that. If you want to be free you can't
draw a circle around yourself and declare all else out of bounds.
He understood that if he didn't take care of his wife the feeling
of impotence would effectively neuter him for the rest of his days.
Certainly the feeling of killing her caused him some discomfort—he
still loved her—but it would leave him in a place where he could live
in peace whatever the circumstances. He could have been wrong;
the crime could have left him wracked with guilt and remorse, even
self-loathing; in which case, his choice would have been a mistake.
But he wasn't wrong. The rest of his life was a circus, and he was
a spectator as well as the ringmaster, and he loved it. Of course his
happiness earned him the sobriquet of sociopath, even psychopath,
but he believed, and I agree with him, he had made the right choice,
being who he was. The cut he made on her nerve through which
electricity flowed to her heart was not made in anger, or a desire
for revenge, or punishment, or to cause her pain. It was made out
of an obligation to his own peace of mind, his own happiness. His
lack of remorse stirred up hate in others, to be sure, but that was
to be expected.

If Willie is not to be blamed, neither is the person who took his
life. Willie had lived his life the way he was meant to live it, and
the person who ended it for him was acting in his own interest,
according to his own immutable design. I doubt the harmless old
man seriously objected, other than perhaps about the manner of his

dying. He bled to the last drop, you could see that from the size of the stain.

The window cracks open, and a breeze slips in. I walk over and let the night air caress my face. The last traces of the squall have fled. The moon has gone white as chalk. Even the leaves are quiet. No fluttering of bat wings or shaking of baby rattles. The solitude is creased by the lonely wail of a loon at the far end of the lake.

I close the window. Clarity will bring peace, you think. You hope. But what if it doesn't? There is no going back now. Even to the small town down the road. The world will be catching up to me soon. But the night is still mine, and I will make of it what I will.

The briefcase now sitting alone on the chair by the window was my identity in my teaching days; the more battered it got, the more wisdom it carried within it. In my little plays in the classroom, it had sometimes served as the child on the floor. Never repaired once, I think, over all the years. The splotch on the handle, however, was disconcerting. I reach for the case and lift it by the edge. It's heavier than I thought, and I have to grasp it firmly. I set it on my lap. I rub a finger on the handle, hold it under the lamp, and it comes up dark crimson. I turn my palm over; the streak on it matches the handle. I unsnap the brass clasp. My hand is a little shaky. A book sits in the front slot. In the next slot is a sheaf of papers. In the last one, a small calendar and a newspaper article. The book, I see, is the Professor's memoir, *The Joy of Killing*. I can't help but smile.

After the success of my novel, the Professor undertook to write the story of the killing and the consequences from inside his head. The very personal memoir takes the reader right up to the moment of his execution. It did quite well posthumously and still has quite a following. People respect honesty in others, even if they don't live it themselves.

Since the Professor was dead, I was frequently asked to read from and talk about the book. One campus presentation had drawn over one hundred students. When I was finished reading, there was utter silence, then muted but sustained applause.

I slipped the book from the briefcase. On the back cover is a split screen of the elegant, educated face of the author and a wooden electric chair with straps and a metal cap. That some people took the book literally was not the author's fault. Even the title was criticized for being too provocative. The book was banned from the campus bookstore, suffered a feminist boycott, which only helped its sales.

The Professor understood that he had a choice in killing his wife, and he insisted that he had made the right choice. He was willing to accept the consequences of his action. He had gone happily to his death. He wrote that he looked forward to the experience, and you believed it. But still he wanted to stay conscious as long as possible, to live fully every last second of his dying. I wrote the afterward to the memoir, since I was one of the witnesses to the execution. His eyes slid open after the first jolt. He was saying something; I took it to be "Nothing really matters," although no one else heard this. I wanted that to be the title of the book, but the publisher insisted on *The Joy of Killing*, since the Professor described in such compelling detail the deep satisfaction the severing of his wife's spinal cord brought him. Page after page, and it was this that brought the most objections. You needn't read it, I said. But they had to. I'd heard that people got sick before they could put it down.

THE BELL ON the Underwood bings loudly. It's the first time I've heard the sound all night. I push the lever on the carriage and slide it back along the track, until it catches. I push a key that releases it, and it tears back along the track and bangs to a stop; the bell rings, more loudly this time it seems, as if objecting to the foolishness. I see that I've been writing about the girl on the train. I'm pleased, because I believe even more than before that the story of that night is my road to salvation. I've come some distance as it is. And I believe that the boy need not suffer from it. He can stay as he is, which right now is pretty happy with the way things are going. Whatever shadow hangs over him is unseen and unfelt, which is the way it should be.

I'VE LOCKED EYES with the girl in the mirror. Her head rocks with each push into her, but her eyes don't leave me. Her hands are grasping the sink. My hands hold her hips, my thumbs imprinting brightly, and I want to look down at the sight, but I'm scared to leave her eyes, fearful that I might lose her if I do.

FOR ALL OF his physical dominance—he's a good three inches taller than the girl—the boy understands he's not in control, but it doesn't bother him. In fact, I suspect he's rather grateful. He's beginning to trust the girl. As for her, she's a mystery, isn't she? She's kind to the boy, as if she sees something to love in him, even knowing this night is the end of it. There is a slight air of urgency about her. *She needs something from him.* For a moment I'm distracted by the sounds of our coupling. It's a powerful rhythm, and it seems disconnected from me. My thighs are shaking.

"Slowly," she says.

In the midst of all the sensations, I feel a faint ache. I look away from the mirror. Lights are flashing by outside. We are next to a highway. People in cars going the same way could see us. She rocks her hips gently, and I hold perfectly still. It feels like she's pulling me inside her, all of me. My hands float off her hips and lift her skirt up. I tilt my head back. Burning the image for all time in my brain. Even the red marks from my hands, which now fold the edge of her skirt up over her waist. I lower my head to see what I can see, but sweat creeps into my eyes and stings and blurs. I'm more outside than in, and I freeze on the edge of laughter.

The girl stops moving. "I can't feel you," she says.

I slip almost out, hesitate; I can barely make out the conjunction of our flesh. I hold for a long second, and bang in, thinking let's see if you feel this. She lets out a sharp cry of pleasure and pushes back into me hard, and I get it then—who can take the most, inflict the most, hurt the most. I'm slicked all over and breathing hard. And so it goes. I slam into her, she cries out, then pushes hard back into me, at which point I must hold straight and solid as a post. And back and forth we go, until the rhythm is consuming, and the train rocks and click-clacks in time with us, and it seems like we could roll on like this through the night.

I wonder if in that moment some healing began. There was no thinking, or observing, no separation. The energy flowed back and forth between them, like a powerful, releasing balm. Finally, he lets go. Tears slide down his cheeks, land on her bottom.

BING! THE BELL goes. A half page has gone by. I nod my head. The kid was doing all right, for a beginner. He's a natural. At least this night. I push the carriage to the right. I close my eyes, to play out the rest of the scene, my fingers skipping over the keys.

MY EYES SWING over to *The Joy of Killing*. Bright red letters on white. The Professor's memoir was quite remarkably stitched together, a compellingly told story from inside the mind of a remorseless killer. Hard to believe he was an academic. In my novel, he had earned a second PhD in anthropology, and his study in this area greatly affected his philosophy. His initial area of focus had been the early crop civilizations in the Fertile Crescent, when man had learned to plant wheat and rye, which meant that he could store them and take the winter off. It allowed him to settle down and not spend all of his time hunting for his next meal. He had time for art and music and community. He began painting and writing stories and composing music, which gave him memory and hope and capacities beyond simple survival. It also gave him time to develop a broader range of emotional strategies beyond reduction of fear and procreation. He began to possess a woman, rather than just breed her out of instinct. He had his own home, his own plot of land, and now he had the time and energy to fight to protect them. The freedom to act from pure instinct had been lost by this shift. Emotional strategies were woven into all behavior now;

anger became the critical feeling, for it drove the various forms
of violence, retaliation, and retribution. Theft. Assault. Murder.
Rape. The primitive mind began evolving into a process of weaving
instincts into emotional landscapes. It had to. If a neighbor began
sleeping with your wife, you were more effective if you responded
with anger; you would do a better job of making him pay in a
way that would discourage him or anyone else from doing it again.
Even better if you could make him feel guilty over what he did. If
his wife and children shamed him for it. If he felt remorse over it.
Instinct, while critical, was no longer the linchpin. And if you slept
with his wife, you predicted—and here was the key element of the
Professor's doctoral thesis and subsequent scholarly efforts—you
predicted that you would not feel bad for having done it; or rather,
that the joy you felt while and after screwing her would far outweigh any negative feelings, such as guilt at having used the woman
to get even with the man. Predicting correctly is the definition of
wisdom.

Under the Professor's theory, the reason I failed to stick an ice
pick in the back of my first wife was because I understood that the
momentary joy arising from having committed the most forbidden
of all acts would not hold up; it would be ruined by feelings of guilt
and self-loathing and eventually the worst of them all—regret. So I
didn't do it, but not because I'm some moral human being, superior
to the sociopathic killer, but because I know myself. We are both
acting true to our nature.

I would have to agree with the Professor in most respects. I
never felt tempted to take violent action against Willie, or David,

for that matter, because I could not envision myself receiving much joy from it. Perhaps relief, a sense of closure, even a somewhat transient sense of contentment. Certainly nothing even close to overcoming the consequential feelings, nothing to stand up to the judgment of others—my friends and family, the world. I would pass the remaining days in misery, of this I was sure. Does this make me a sociopath? To refrain from violence because I sense my incapability to deal with the emotional aftermath? To find peace from the act? To maintain a sliver of joy for what would remain of my life? To me it is utterly rational.

The difficulty I encountered was that so many people assumed that I was like the Professor. Because I wrote a novel based on his story, and then supported the publication of his memoir and stood up and explained—I did not defend it, exactly—the Professor's theory of violence, people assumed that I agreed with and supported the killing of his wife. I understand it, I would say, which is a far piece from saying *I agree with what he did*. The dean insisted that I condemn the murder as wrong or amoral or evil, which, for the reasons I've set forth above, I could not in good conscience do. Nature versus nurture is in essence a specious argument. Others have written that the biology of the brain is involved in the wiring of criminal minds—to what extent we are not sure—and environmental factors make up the rest of the story. What else is there?

When I taught a course on *The Joy of Killing*, I struggled to set out the simplest concepts of the Professor's theory free and clear of emotional entanglements or ideology. Without much success, I must confess. I would ask the students: What difference does it make if the behavior of the brutal killer results from an inferior amygdala or being sexually assaulted in his childhood? It's all nature, is it not? Human behavior stems from the same source as animal behavior, I pointed out. I would tell the story of the ape who tore a woman's face off in the laboratory. I would note that the ape, like the brutal killer, is responsible for neither the design of his brain nor the confluence of the social factors beating in on the formation of it. You cannot judge the killer any more than you can judge the ape. The dean agreed in principle, but he refused to back down from his insistence that I stop teaching the theory and condemn the Professor for the good of the college, which by now was in a total uproar. You simply can't say that there's nothing wrong with murdering your wife for sleeping with your neighbor, he insisted. What I saw in the dean's eyes was the possibility that I myself was like the Professor, that I myself might have no difficulty in murdering my wife if I caught her fucking someone. (Which I hadn't done, of course, but I couldn't tell him that.) That's what scared him, and the others, that evil lurked behind my very eyes, and perhaps theirs as well.

It seldom helped to explain our theory of human motivation to critics: that people acted solely on their prediction of the emotional outcomes of their behavior. I would pick a simple, innocuous example. You're out for a walk on a hot summer day and you come to an ice cream stand with an inviting presentation of flavors. You appear to decide not to have a cone because of your diet. But the process is likely more complex and subtle than that as you balance out the emotional consequences. If I eat an ice cream cone, I will have a good feeling at the time. However, in not too long I will crash from the sugar, and I will feel bad from having eaten an unhealthy thing, from having wasted the money, from consuming the calories. You weigh in your mind whether the enjoyment from eating the ice cream cone will in the end outweigh the crash and the guilt. Which isn't to say that you might not end up making an emotionally stupid decision; that while you know that the negative consequences will far outweigh the rush, you go for the short term and eat the ice cream anyway. Another factor in the equation: you learn from experience that if you don't buy the ice cream cone you will be entitled to the good feelings of self-control and self-righteousness. The key, of course, is learning to accurately predict the emotional consequences, and to act according to the prediction. The Professor believed, as did I, that this process, to whatever extent conscious or unconscious, was behind every decision human beings made. In his case, as I said, he correctly predicted that the joy he felt from murdering his wife would far outweigh the consequences he would suffer from the act. Conversely, he understood the terrible feelings that would afflict him if he did not take care of her. So, he ended up in balance. Call it what else you will. The students continued to insist, however, that their decisions were made strictly on a rational, conscious consideration of all the facts.

I push the book aside and think back to the boy and the girl in the vestibule on the train. He is still in a state of rigidity from the orgasm—except that his legs are weakening.

THE LAST OF me has drained inside the girl. Her head is low and I can't see her eyes, but she seems to be shaking, too. I pull halfway out and plunge back in. She looks up at me, an almost desperate longing on her face. She reaches back and grabs my hand from her hip and places a finger between the lips of her pussy, moves it back and forth, and then drops her hand. I feel a little embarrassed, but the feel of the nub under my finger shoots juice into my brain and steadies me. I am the male, again. Her fate lay with me, the skill of my finger. I catch the reflection in the mirror. The scar on my thigh glistens. I rub the nub back and forth, slowly and lightly, until I feel her impatience, and then I bear down until it slips away. Then as fast and hard as I can, pausing every few seconds, until I can begin to feel a sound rising in her throat. I pinch the nub between my fingers.

SEE HOW EASILY I get lost in the narrative? The power of the scene overwhelms me so if I'm not careful I might stay in it and perhaps never resurface. The image of the last few moments, when I could see from her eyes that she was finally done, could keep me in thrall for a long time. I'm tempted to give in and let it be the final scene in my head—no one would ever know the difference—but then my life would have ended perhaps in a confabulation, certainly in confusion, and the feeling that accompanies clarity—at least the one I *predict* will accompany clarity—will have been forever lost to me. The feeling of not clinging to life is one of great freedom, beyond what I could ever have imagined, but it comes only with the understanding that your entire psyche is fair game. Reluctantly, I let the girl's face in the mirror fade from my vision, knowing the next time I see her the explosion will have evaporated and the hard aftermath will be facing us; which, right now, I barely remember.

In the darkness, I wait. It seems there's a shadow in my mind. The projector has broken. Or the reel is empty. Ironic: how I longed for this during the course of my life, simple moments of darkness, where the present was unimpeded by images real or unreal of the past, and I could simply *be*. Not to say that it never happened, but other than times when I was on something or other it was pretty rare. Even in my sleep I seldom found peace. Seconds slip by. I think of times and places to generate a flash. I turn once again to the girl on the train, I try to taste her, smell her, touch her, but now she is dim at best, a faint hologram of an image. The detectives. My mother. David. Even the wretch Willie. Thoughts of them pass through my mind, unaccompanied by the images that will make me feel something and kick the narrative into flow. I haven't time for the numbness to wear off, have I? If I had a match, I would light it and hold it under a finger. If I had a knife, I would slice open a knuckle. My hand suddenly reaches for the briefcase; in the bottom is a zipper leading to a hidden compartment in which I sometimes kept pills and other times photographs, or recently, after the publication of *The Professor* and *The Joy of Killing*, a knife. A knife with a long thin blade meant to slice not cut, the very one I had seen in the drying rack on the kitchen counter this morning. Which means it's probably not in the briefcase. I jerk the briefcase up to my lap, open it, and tap along the bottom, where the zipper is hidden under a thin fold of leather. Something is in there. I open the fold with one hand and pull the zipper down with the other. There is the black riveted handle. I touch it lightly, as if it is a sacred object. I pry open the leather flap further, to see the blade. What a beauty. I used it as a prop when describing the Professor's crime of murder. In front of the class I would hold the knife lightly, where it seemed no more than a feather, and balance it on one finger. It was sharp enough to shred paper.

The Professor confessed at the trial that the instance in the hammock wasn't the first time he had caught his wife and his neighbor cheating; about a week earlier, through a window in the next-door garage, he had seen his wife spread out like a doll on the workbench, her hands and ankles cleated to the wood, while the neighbor crouched on elbows and knees and hammered into her. At the trial, he introduced a video of them screwing on the dock of the pavilion on City Lake, under the moonlight, with a radio playing next to a half-empty bottle of wine. In between incidents, the Professor sharpened the knife and waited for what he felt would be the propitious moment, when all would have tilted in the direction of the end he predicted. Thus, he admitted he had planned it. There was no irresistible impulse. No heat of passion. He begged for nothing from the jury. He just wanted them to feel everything he had felt, leading up to, during, and after the murder, so they would understand the common sense nature of the act.

The Professor, with a shock of black hair graying at the temples, wearing horn-rimmed glasses, stood at the bar in a tweed jacket and slacks and spoke to the members of the jury in his genteel manner, as if they were a class of his brightest students. You could see them gradually get it, and several of them, women, surprisingly, began nodding along, particularly when he got to the point in the theory about the ability of people to accurately predict which line of behavior would lead to which emotional consequences. For men, he explained, image is critical to how they feel about themselves; not image in so much as looks, but as in masculinity, meaning competitiveness. To be outwitted by a man in a business deal, or to lose his wife to the neighbor down the block, will leave him feeling like a loser in the eyes of the world, and in his own eyes, certainly a feeling to be avoided if at all possible.

Women, on the other hand, care little about winning or losing or how they appear in the eyes of the world; what matters to them is their internal feelings about themselves. Am I a decent human being? Am I a kind and caring person, sensitive to the needs of others? She will not confront the person who cuts in the movie line because she doesn't want to feel like a bully. Both men and women modify their behavior in ways to maximize the good feelings and minimize the bad ones.

It might be hard to accept, the Professor told the jurors, but there is no such thing as a truly unselfish act. The woman who volunteers ten hours a week at the Animal Rescue Foundation does so for the simple reason that it makes her feel like a good person. The man who coaches the boys' soccer team does so because it provides him the opportunity to obtain the feeling of winning. The philanthropist who donates millions of dollars a year to girls' education in the countries of sub-Saharan Africa does so because the magnitude of the gift will demonstrate to one and all that he is indeed a male at the top of the heap, and that will provide the feeling he has sought for as long as he can remember.

So, you see me here before you today, the Professor told the jury, a man who acted according to his true nature. I do not ask for your forgiveness, nor do I ask for you leniency. I ask only for your understanding. I loved my wife. I miss her to this day. But had I allowed her to live I would have become a fraudulent human being, an unbearable fate to which no one should knowingly consign himself. The choice I made was the choice I had to make. I know you will make yours with the same integrity.

To everyone's surprise, the jury was out for two days before bringing in a guilty verdict.

I notice the typewriter has long since fallen silent. This meandering of the mind is wasteful, and this path was particularly nonproductive. It's been five years since I quit the college, and I thought I had left most of this behind. I haven't spoken or written about *The Joy of Killing* or the Professor himself for several years. I don't disavow him, but I am not him. It was an exercise in philosophical and mental expansion, meant to test the limits of people's tolerance. That there might be some truth to it is really no longer the point. I've never lived according to the principles, and I don't regret it. The point now is to finish the night's work.

I PICK UP the knife, determined to put it away and get on with the story of the girl on the train. Along the top edge I notice a faint smear of what appears to be blood. I am startled. I don't remember putting the knife in the case, yet I was sure I saw it in the dish holder this morning. It was clean then.

Could I have killed Willie? Absolutely not. Such an act would have stayed with me in vivid detail. I hadn't thought about the man for years until I read the article in the paper this morning.

I can smell the aftershave now as if I was in his room. He is sitting on the bed, with David next to him. Willie was trying to put on a pleasant face, but lust had contorted it.

I am still as stone in front of the table, fighting the realization that I had always been aware that this was what it was all about. How could you look at Willie and not know what he was up to? David glanced at me—and I see this for the first time now—smiled a small guilty smile. An admission of deceit, complicity. Willie's grubby little hand moved from David's thigh to his groin, dug in, tugged the zipper down, and disappeared. Willie's face clenched in pleasure as he grasped the prize, and his thin lips worked and moistened. I could not get up and leave. I had to watch. David's eyes were closed, whether in pleasure or disgust, I didn't know, but suddenly I wondered if David was the way Willie was and all this talk of girls was bullshit. Willie's mouth descended on David. An ugly sound emanated from the man. His head moved slowly up and down. I couldn't watch the rest of it. I stood and moved toward the door. I turned the lock and pulled it open. David glanced over at me.

A CAR HORN sounded from below. I jumped. The knife clattered to the floor. It sounded again. I rose and walked to the window at the back of the room, facing out over the drive and porch. It was the caretaker's dark blue Dodge van. Had he come to confront me? Joseph was his only son. Sally, I gathered, had never married; he was an old man with no grandchildren. The look in his eyes earlier was speckled with pain, an old man's pain, perhaps, but still capable of fueling violence.

The driver's door on the van opened. Two feet swung out, hit the ground, and a figure straightened. It was not the caretaker. A woman. Tall and with coal black hair. After all this time, I recognized her. The confidence of her posture. The tilt of her head. Sally glanced up at the window. Her beauty was effervescent in the moonlight. She walked to the back of the van, opened the door, leaned in, and straightened up with a cardboard box in her arms. Without looking up again, she walked to the porch and set it down. She moved back to the car. I grabbed the handles on the window and pulled up. Jammed tight. I undid the lock on the top of the bottom window and jerked again, without success. I raised my hands to rap on the window, but she was getting in the car, and it was too late, and it shouldn't happen anyway. The world inside this room at the top of the house overlooking the lake contained my fate. I was sure the box sitting on the porch was meant for me. I watched the van pull out of the drive, under the clean light of the white moon, and disappear into the trees at the turn of the road. Sally had never left this town, or her brother, behind. She never would.

THE GIRL AND I sat in the vestibule in the train car and stared out the window at the lights and passing towns. She was loosely in my arms. I breathed in her scent. I wasn't sure what to do or say now. There seemed a kind of sadness about her. About us. As if the rough passion had sucked the spirit out of us, and now that the night was over we would drift slowly apart, like two canoes on a placid lake.

She turned to me. "Where did you grow up?"

"In a small town in Iowa. You?"

"Chicago, North Shore."

Her eyes were misty. "What was it like growing up in your house?"

I had to think for a second. "Not much fun."

"Why?"

"Everyone's waiting for the next explosion, from my mother."

"Your father, too?"

"He went along with the show. The path of least resistance."

Like me, I should have added. I went along with things, too. For all the trouble I've been in, it was never my idea.

I didn't tell her this. I don't think I even knew it myself back then. Christmas, my childhood, wasn't that bad. I don't want to overplay it, suggest by sleight of hand that that's why I've lead such a disjointed life and ended up here, alone, in my little refuge. I did what I wanted, and didn't do what I didn't want. In the face of my mother's tirades, I went numb. I never took anything as absolutely what it seemed. In the train car that evening, having just had my first sexual experience, with a girl way out of my league, even then I wasn't that sure of the reality of it all; even then it felt like I was beginning to make parts of it up, fill in the space and glaze over the dull parts. I looked at the girl's forehead and realized that it wasn't blood on the skin, but lipstick from the mirror. She had run into her own word. What else had I painted into the scene over the years?

"It doesn't matter?" I said.

"What doesn't?" she asked.

"Your forehead," I said. "The red lipstick."

She sat up and glanced in the mirror. She laughed.

"It was my first time," I said before I could stop myself. I looked at her. "First time all the way."

She leaned in, kissed me lightly on the lips. She lay her head on my shoulder, touched my neck. "I like you," she said.

I CLOSE MY eyes to recreate the scene. It was almost as exciting as the sex. She loved what she saw, and she saw more than either of us admitted. Somehow she understood, I could feel it, and the sensation was so strong it scared me.

I TURN THE light off and stand slowly. When my eyes adjust to the dark, I step to the window. I see that the moon has floated just beyond the center of the night sky and is now so dominant it eclipses the stars and planets. The limbs and leaves of the great oaks have fallen invisible. The lake beneath the moon reflects the light back into the sky, accentuating its power. I can feel the pull of the orb in my blood. I am strong. My sight is extremely sharp; I can make out the ripples in the middle of the lake. I can hear the waves wash over the rocks below. The night is now half over, and it's mine, I see that now. It belongs to me. Everything lay before me like a kingdom before a king. In this light there are no shadows, no place to hide. Everything will be revealed. I will fly into the night free and feel nothing more than the cool air on my brow. This feeling of freedom is the one I believed would befall me when I approached understanding of the lines of my life. The clouds are clearing, the water is calming, the blood is flowing smoothly and cleanly through my veins, enlivening my organs, for the final vision. How it turned out, I no longer cared. The girl, I thought, her true beauty lay in her understanding, in her sight. Feeling that now, at this moment, in the power of the moon, has brought me here, as I predicted, without knowing quite how.

An image of the knife slips unbidden from the shadow of the moon. The absolute glory of the moment is gone, and I am slightly pissed over it, but wisely I let the feeling go, and a gradual sensation of calm falls over me as I let the moonlight wrap me in its silvery embrace. I breathe even more deeply until I can feel the squecze of the heart pulse the blood through my groin. With a finger I wipe the lipstick from the girl's forehead and make a cross with it on mine. She laughs and touches my cheek, and the last of my resistance gives way.

Thunk! I jump back, startled. Something smashed into the window. Dropped to the windowsill. There is a faint stain on the glass. I lift the latch and push open the window. The night air is sharp and powerful. My hands and arms are so white in the moonlight I can see the blue veins, the magic disc so bright I can barely look into it. A dark form lays crumpled on the ledge below the window. Little black eyes stare blindly at the moon. A wing flutters in despair. I remember that bats flew in packs of thousands; this one must have lost his way, confused by the brightness of the light. I poke its wing gently. Its tiny furry body heaves jerkily. Still alive, I think. Just stunned. I lean over and lift the wing and stretch it out to full span. The tiny black struts arch in response. The skin is translucent; through it I can see blurry moonlight. The wing, half a foot at least, twitches from my finger and folds back in. The mouth pops open to reveal two fangs. Beyond myth, I know, there is such a thing as bloodsucking bats that feed on people and animals. I look closer: two smaller teeth arc up from the bottom to intersect nicely with the top ones. The glassy eyes don't blink, but I swear they move slightly in my direction. I pull my hand back, and the tiny mouth clenches. I am tempted to brush him from the ledge, to see if it would bring him around and he could gain flight. I want to see him fly off and sweep across the face of the moon with his cohorts, taking with him my touch on his wings. The thought makes me shiver. I close the window quietly and turn away.

WILLIE OR THE UNDERWOOD

FOR A MOMENT I'm caught in the irony: all the blood in this story—on my hand, jeans, the paper, the cat whiskers, not to mention Shelley Duvall—and I spotted not a drop on the fangs of the bat. I need to calm down and get back to work, back to the girl on the train. Always the girl on the train. I settle into the chair. The metal space bar on the Underwood, I notice for the first time, is severely worn in the middle. Various thumbs must have tapped it millions of times to cause the crease. I tap it with my left thumb, then my right. I accept the Professor's principle of human motivation: your choice always anticipates an emotional payoff. In small things—you pour your vodka over ice because you believe that chilled vodka will be more pleasing than straight vodka; and big things—you choose to marry a particular woman not because you love her but because the feeling of someone else having her is intolerable. A man debates whether to go to a funeral of a brother he didn't care for, and he asks: How bad will I feel if I don't go? I would estimate—and this is the subject of my never-to-be-finished paper, the one scattered about on my living room floor, that at least 80 percent of all human behavior is aimed at *avoiding* feelings; the main ones being guilt, shame, or regret. No one wants to feel bad about what they did with their life, so they do what they think they need to do to avoid that feeling at the end. Almost always unsuccessfully, I might add. Very few people feel good about their lives at the end, if they feel anything at all. The Professor was one of them. I will be one, once I come through the fog of this story. And that's all I want: a decent feeling at the end. Over the years I've thought about the girl and that night on the train because it brings me pleasure, more pleasure than most of my relationships, in fact. There was no dishonesty, and she saw the truth, whether she could articulate it or not, and it's that truth I would have her share with me. There is no other source of it; Joseph is dead; Willie is dead; my first wife is dead. The Professor is dead. I hear a flutter of wings. I step to the window, just in time to see the bat arch his wings and swoop down from the ledge. He rises above the treetops, into the sky, the white light of the moon. He streaks across the face of it.

The stars have receded into tiny specks. This means that time is growing short; in not too long, the fading of the black around the edges will toll the hour. I dare not rush the story, but I must focus on moving through the thin shrouds of memory or else the opportunity will be lost. I relax and take a deep breath.

I remember bumping my shoulder on the corner of Willie's dresser as I left the room. I glanced back a final time as I closed the door, and I saw the sight that is so clear in my mind now. Willie's glasses have fallen off and lay on the floor next to his shoes. His thin hair, slicked back, is curled on his collar. David's hand is resting easily on his shoulder. I pulled the door shut behind me. Outside the window at the end of the hall, I can see children playing in the yard. The walls in the hallway are greasy, the carpet thin and torn. I jammed my hands in my pocket and bolted for the stairways. As I turned on the step, the door to the first apartment opened open a crack, and I saw the face of the old lady who had been watching us from the window earlier. Her door closed soundlessly. I was dizzy when I finally hit the front door. I leaned into the fresh air. The children were screaming now.

As the boy steps onto the sidewalk, I notice a look of confusion on his face. The scene must still be in his head, like a painting on a rock wall. Yet I've never seen it before. Only vague recollections of the apartment building, the playground, even the hallway. The image must have disintegrated slowly, into bits and pieces, slivers. I could see how it would fuck him up some, being made a fool of like that. He hadn't done anything except watch, and leave, and yet I can see that he feels dirty himself. Is this where it started, I think? The learning of the ability to disintegrate stories into images and images into bits and pieces, molecules, even, protons, which barely recognize each other, and which float unmolested and free form in the subcutaneous consciousness. Some forever unseen; others to collide in new and vibrant images, which may or may not have the slightest to do with the original event. It's a way of being, and one of which I think the Professor would approve, for it is essentially honest. There is nothing to measure your self against, because your self doesn't really exist as a thing. You can't argue the truth of anything to anybody; you can't in good conscience pass judgment on anyone, even yourself. If you live it through and through, if you don't strive for some objective picture of life, you will accept the existence of all things as emanations of nature. *You won't struggle.* Obviously I never got there, or I wouldn't be here, at my desk, knocking out letters on the keys of an ancient Underwood and thinking of the night I spent with the girl on the train. And yet I don't think of my childhood as particularly disjointed. Alone, yes, but not miserable. The observer, the thinker, the describer— who even then understood as some sort of cognitive birthright that nothing really mattered, not in the slightest, and could sense the freedom such an understanding could bring if he could accept it with every breath. He got into trouble, yes, as I've mentioned, but not because he was angry or rebellious, but mainly because down deep he didn't care. He went along with the others and shoplifted and broke school windows and skipped class and swiped his grand-mother's car. Because it was something to do and all the same to him. The meetings in the principal's office, the sessions down at the Booneville Police Department, the threats from juvenile probation officers registered, but didn't hold his mind in place. He was unto himself, it seems. So, the way I see it now, he had barely retrieved his bike from behind the drugstore and swung over the bar for the ride home when the disintegration of the scene in Willie's room began.

Somewhere growing up the boy came to understand the void you would be left in if you truly lived according to this principle. You would, for all intents and purposes, be alone. Which really shouldn't matter, but the truth was he didn't like the feeling of being all alone. So, in accordance with the Professor's theory of motiva-tion (he didn't see it this way at the time, of course) he learned to behave in a way that would alleviate, if not avoid, this feeling of aloneness. It worked, to some extent. He kept his views to him-self. He became deft at acting as if one thing or another mattered, whether some new film was a director's greatest yet, what grade he got in geology class, if Rocky Marciano was going to retain the World Heavyweight title. That was his state when he met the girl on the train; she was beautiful and sexy and on the face of it unlikely to want to have much to do with him, but he went along with her because he knew it would feel good if he did, and it did feel good; she felt good. As you can tell, he was worried and anxious, but he felt the joy of the pleasures of her body and the power of her needing him, and he altered his behavior in order to obtain more of it, and he avoided behaving in ways that he thought might end up depriving him of it, and in the course of the night he even experienced feelings of deep affection for her, of love, you might say. He was greatly pleased with the discovery of this capacity within himself. But did he ever believe that it really mattered? That the experience meant something? He might have, at the time, I'll cede that. And even now I see it as probably the emotional highlight of his life. If I could have seen ways through my life to replicate the feelings of that night, I would have. But even then I would not have believed that it mattered, not in any substantive way. The desire to seek emotional depth was based on the simple belief that it would be more satisfying than the absence of it, of emotional shallowness. Nothing more. The true value of the night on the train, as I've said before, lies in my belief that within it exists the portal to some sort of linear understanding of a few key events in my life. I guess it does matter, but only in the sense that being allowed to die in some sort of peace matters. Could I swear that I had always seen life this way, even before the morning at Willie's apartment building? No, of course not. Who could know anything about their childhood for sure? But I see the boy now, on his much beloved green-and-white Schwinn, pedaling off to the municipal swimming pool, seemingly neutral toward the day and all things.

I have no doubt that Willie was murdered out of someone's emotional need. The rip up the man's throat into his jawbone was not a robber's act. David, perhaps? I started to write that, if so, I hoped he felt a release from some intolerable feeling. Then I wasn't so sure. Perhaps I hoped that it made him feel worse, having waited all these years, and only lately finding the guts to be a murderer. Like I said, my mother prohibited any further contact with David, and besides that I began to see him as a possible Willie-in-the-making.

WE HAD DRIFTED off in each other's arms when the loud rapping sounded on the vestibule door. Behind it this time was a male voice. "Open the door," it said. "Other people need to use the bathroom." The girl looked at me. Her face was soft, pillowy. She looked gentle and kind and hot, like an adolescent Anita Ekberg.

"Shall we let them in?" she asked.

"Let's not," I said, knowing the moment would be lost.

"Just a moment," she called. "I'm cleaning up."

To which there was no reply.

I can see the conductor with the wire-rimmed, round glasses and the blue vest assembled by a vertical line of brass buttons, his boney fist poised to knock again, and the old lady behind him with her small mouth pursed and her eyes anxiously focused on the door. I stared in silent fascination as the girl rearranged herself—shifting her skirt around so the zipper was on the side, reaching under her sweater and buttoning her blouse, straightening the little white collar, running her fingers through her hair until it fell loosely to her shoulders. She kissed me on the forehead. "Be right back," she said and slipped into the tiny toilet. I stood, zipped up, and straightened my pants around. I looked in the mirror; same me, but my hair was a mess, and there was a faint red cross on my forehead and a low-wattage glow in my eyes. I ran my hands through my hair but decided to leave the stain alone.

I heard the twirling of a roll of toilet paper. Then the blast of the lid as it snapped open, silence as it snapped shut. The door opened and she stood there, hands at her sides, looking at me, clearly pleased. The pleat in the very front of her skirt was creased sideways, and I reached and pulled it until it fell straight. She pressed herself against my hand. I pressed back until I could feel the cleft of her.

"You're quite the guy," she said, glancing at my forehead. "Red cross and all."

My hand fell away. I thought to myself, for all that's happened I haven't seen down there. I've no idea know what it looks like. No idea. She read me. "It's still a long way to Chicago."

The knocking sounded again, this time louder. "Let's go, in there, you two."

She straightened my shirt, patted the soft bulge in my pants, looked at herself once more in the mirror, and opened the door.

I wish I had a painting of that scene. In the middle of the doorway, the conductor's face was scrunched between fervent curiosity and moral revulsion. Slightly behind him, peering over his shoulder, was the lady, her face taught with bitter disapproval, disgust possibly. They both looked us up and down, as if we might be naked or sotted in something unmentionable.

"Excuse me," the girl said, and just then the train jolted and tilted her toward the conductor, and he raised his arms and caught her. She held there in his arms, for a second or two. She brushed in closer as she turned toward the aisle. I followed in her path, feeling the woman's harsh eyes on me assuming, I guess, that I was the wrong doer.

I FEEL LIKE we're finally getting somewhere. The bones are loosening in my head, my fingers are jumping from one key to the next. The images are hooking together more securely, as if they might truly belong in this sequence and in this coloration forever. I breathe in deeply and roll my shoulders. The tear in my jeans, the gash and the blood, doesn't matter anymore. The knife. All bits and pieces of some mysterious metaphor, not necessary for me to decipher. Today is not the point, is it? Yesterday, yesteryear (as the voice in *The Lone Ranger* would intone), holds the answer. From that, all else will certainly clear up. I have to say, though, I'm a bit concerned about the brass buttons on the conductor's vest. First time they've appeared. I could have forgotten them, which would be preferable to having added them in this latest version. I close my eyes; yes, the watch chain is still there, flowing from right to left, but now thinner and duller and much less impressive. If I had to pick, which I don't, I would go with the buttons on the vest. Now that I think about it, the snapping of the lid on the toilet in the vestibule was something new, as well. She'd disappeared in there, the water closet, to pee, I assumed. Now I believe it was to cleanse herself of my seed. This new reality is unsettling, not so much because of that image, but because I can't help but imagine my seed smeared on a piece of toilet paper, whooshing down the pipe and dropping onto the rocks below. To disintegrate, but perhaps not; perhaps to calcify on a rock, or fossilize on some lonely stretch of track between there and the end of the line.

I am pleased with the progress—the next scene with the girl on the train seems to hold tremendous promise, although I couldn't tell you at this moment why—and thus I'm not greatly annoyed when that disturbing noise sounds again from the bottom of the stairs. I listen carefully, and there it is again: a rattling sound, like what might emanate from a large and vociferous rattlesnake. Both doors are locked, I know that; if I have to I'll crawl out the window, stand on the ledge, and pee. To hell with him, rattle on. I'm on the road; I'm on the way. It occurs to me that perhaps that is what Sally left in the box below, a snake. But I had heard the sound before she came here. Perhaps now there are two of them. Let it be, if that's the case. If it made her feel better to scare me, where's the harm? As for the dragging sound, I couldn't speculate.

SALLY COULD HAVE gone across the lake with Joseph that afternoon, the last day of his life. Maybe she would have convinced him to stay on the opposite shore, at the girl's camp, until the storm passed. But he wouldn't have been able to hustle the brunette with her around. Which is why he wanted me. I wouldn't get in his way. So I went, I've no doubt of that now. I can feel the muscles in my shoulder pulling as I stroke from the front seat of the canoe. The sun was hitting my forehead, which meant it was early afternoon (which resolves that question). I've pulled the straps so tight on the vest that it constricts my breathing. "Switch sides!" Joseph calls out from the rear seat every few minutes or so, and we manage without missing a stroke. The water is smooth, and we slice through it like a knife. By the time we arrive at the camp, I am feeling better about my decision to cross. Standing on the shore, as if they knew we were coming, are two girls: the slender brunette with the dark eyes and flirty smile, and the shorter redhead, with freckles and blue eyes. I hadn't counted on this, on her. I couldn't think of her name. The brunette waved as we approached. Joseph stood up and lifted the paddle over his head, as if we had accomplished some miraculous feat in crossing the lake. The brunette clapped her hands. The redhead smiled.

Joseph's girlfriend was carrying a blanket and a small basket, and the redhead had a brown paper sack in her hand. I could only imagine the promises that had been made to get her here. Joseph winked, said they would be back in about an hour, and off the couple walked, down a path into the woods, hand in hand. The other girl and I stood there awkwardly for a few moments, until she explained that the rest of the camp had gone on a field trip and that her friend had claimed she was sick so she could stay behind. It was her day off from the kitchen. Her lips moved quite deliberately as they formed the words, and her eyes stayed right on mine, as if to make sure I was following what she was saying.

"How'd you get roped into this?" I finally asked.

"When Jeannie asked me to come with her, I said I would but only if she promised that you would come with Joseph."

I flushed. "That's really nice," I said finally, thinking that explains why he was so insistent that I come along. This girl must like me.

"You don't remember my name, do you?"

I shook my head. "Sorry."

"That's OK. JoRene. One word, with a capital R."

JoRene, I say aloud. JoRene. I repeat it several times and then type it in all caps. JORENE. I push the scene along in my head. She told me that her dad cut down trees for a living and her mom was a waitress. She had two brothers and one sister. Do they all have red hair? I asked. She blushed; no, she was the only one in the family. She wanted to go to college, become a school teacher, and move to Minneapolis. I liked her attitude: life need not be complicated, just make a plan. After eating our sandwiches, we walked along the shore. She reached for my hand. When she stopped and turned to me, with chin uplifted, I began talking about the tree swing back at the river and how best to jump off. I could see the disappointment in her eyes. She knew it wasn't there, would never be there.

I remember feeling terrible then, and I feel terrible now, thinking about it. By the time we returned to the dock, we were out of words. We sat in two wooden chairs and waited for the others, and finally, with tears in her blue eyes, she said it was time for her to go. I tried to kiss her good-bye, but she would have none of it.

I watched with concern as a patch of darkness appeared in what had been a bright blue sky, in the center of the lake, right where we would have to paddle. Joseph and the girl finally appeared from the path, unconcerned about anyone but themselves, Joseph wearing a cocky, self-satisfied smile, she with her blouse half-unbuttoned and carrying a basket. "She got away?" he called when he noticed I was by myself. The girl laughed.

I pointed toward the sky. A bad sea was coming. "Look."

Joseph shrugged. "You gotta drive, man. I'm beat." The two exchanged flirty glances.

By that he meant I would take the steering seat, in the back, which was the more difficult position and which he always took.

"We can't go out there," I said. "It's gonna get bad. Someone needs to come get us. I'll call my dad."

"Easy, boy, easy. We'll make it with no problem. I've been through worse."

The girl, now not so happy, chimed in. "They'll kick me out if they catch you guys here."

I should have stayed there, I think. My dad would have come to pick us up. It was our canoe. Mom would have lectured me, maybe grounded me for a day. It wasn't my idea to paddle here in the first place. I knew what Joseph would do, though; his face told me he would tell everyone back at the river that I was a chicken; not only that but that I hadn't gotten anywhere with the girl. The chicken part would ruin whatever chance there was with Sally. Not only that, I would feel like a chicken. That's what nailed me; that feeling was about as bad it gets for a boy, one to be avoided at all costs, even risking your life.

"You're steering," I said.

"All right," he cheered. "Let's get going." He moved to the canoe, edged it into the water.

I tugged on my orange vest, fastened the straps, and picked up a paddle from the sand.

"You gotta have a vest," I said. "Get one from the shed."

He shrugged again.

The girl got it. She rushed to the shed and returned with one in her hands.

"No way to get it back," he said. "People will think I'm a thief." His laugh went right along with the shrug. He turned to her, pulled her in, kissed her long and deep, let a hand drift down over her ass. He winked at me.

I took another look at the lake. The darkness was pulling together into a thick blanket, and it was deepening, so you could no longer see through it, hovering over the water. It was possible to go around it, but it would take longer, and the squall could move anyway. I debated taking the backseat myself. I would take fewer chances than Joseph. If the stern man failed, you were likely to swamp in a storm because you couldn't keep the canoe headed into the waves. My shoulders had stiffened from the paddle over, and I had taken a splinter in my right hand. We were both about six feet, but he was the stronger paddler. His attitude was the problem. He paused at the water's edge, holding the canoe in place, giving me a last chance to take the stern seat. He must be tired, to give up center stage, I thought, and that almost convinced me. But I shook my head and climbed over the edge of the canoe and settled in the front seat. I pulled my straps tight and reached for the paddle. Over my shoulder I saw Joseph pause and look out over the water. We're not going, I thought, but in an instant he was pushing the canoe from the sand and clambering over the edge and into the seat. He raised the paddle overhead and called to the girl, who waved back, the orange life jacket clutched by her side.

AT ONE POINT, everybody in the room was smoking, I remember that. My parents, the two detectives, and myself. All different brands. River scar had lit a Camel, the other guy a long Chesterfield. My parents had Marlboros going. After the first cop used the silver lighter, I pulled the Zippo from my left pocket and clinked it open. His eyes tracked the Marine Corps emblem on the side, my thumb sliding over the globe.

"You want to be a Marine?"

In front of my father I could only say, "Yeah," although he had never pressed me on it.

"You won't make it if we put down here that you lied to police officers."

I waited for my father, who had earned a Silver Star, two Bronze stars, and two Purple Hearts in the Pacific, to say something. I put the unlit cigarette in the ashtray, slipped the Zippo back in my front pocket, and looked out the window.

LOOKING BACK ON that boy, I don't think I could have told them what happened, even if I wanted to. Even if my mother wasn't there, there was no way I could describe the scene. Once on my bike, I pedaled as fast as I could, leaning down over the handlebars to cut the wind, whipping down the street, around corners. Now, looking out the window, with the detectives breathing down my neck, the images had already grown faint, the edges blurry. Which was another reason, if I needed one, to keep my mouth shut. The second cop, with the still eyes and small ears, leaned forward.

"I don't want to be a Marine," I finally said, still looking out the window.

I'd never heard myself say that before. Which really is the whole thing, my coming out here, spending the night with the girl on the train: Who knows what else exists beyond the common mind? Things you've done or said, or have been done or said to you. You can be scared of them most of your life, but if you really want peace of mind you have to allow them to coagulate and simply hope you can handle what comes up. If you understand the nature of the human being, like I do—although I would never take it as far as the Professor—you accept that there is no self that exists independent of the forces that created it, and thus you cannot be held personally, or perhaps I should say morally, accountable for what you did or didn't do. I shouldn't have gone into the apartment building with David and Willie. Perhaps I should have left the minute I saw the leer on Willie's face. Or the moment he unzipped David's pants. Was Willie evil? You tell me. Did he deserve to die the way he did? Probably. Perhaps much earlier, even, and in every bit as bad a way. If he's not evil, then you can't say the person who gutted him was evil. You can't even say he was wrong. Perhaps you would say that Willie had a choice. Bullshit. He had no more choice than the chimp who reached through the bars of his cage and peeled the women's face off. I am always greatly amused by the shows in which the narrator intones profoundly about the great struggle between "man and nature." As if man weren't nature himself, didn't evolve from the same source as the turtle and the typhoon. *I understand* we have to judge and incarcerate and separate in order to have a chance at a civilized society. It's the moral labels we place on the Specks and Pol Pots of the world, as if the fact that we're better than they are is a result of our own doing, that are illegitimate. Pure chance, a simple role of the genetic dice. You deserve no credit or blame for what you do or don't do in your life. If you can breathe this into your soul once and for all, you will experience the freedom of the eagle soaring high over the water. I saw the look of it on the Professor's face as the straps were pulled tight on his chest and legs. He was fully awake to every dimension of the experience; he was hungry for it. When the cap was finally secured to his head, he smiled.

Would I have felt better if I had told the detectives to get fucked right then and there? Perhaps. The good feeling would have lasted until the detectives drove off in their cars and my parents left for a cocktail party at the country club and I was left alone in the house as night fell, and then worse ones would have come over me. Even then, unknowing, I was smart enough to get that. (Not that I give myself credit for it.) Which is where most people fuck up: they mispredict the emotional consequences of what they undertake. Or, more often, more profound, and more sad, they get the feeling they're seeking but it doesn't last. It's faded before a fortnight, and they're right back where they were, or perhaps, as is often the case, worse off. It's as simple as the man who steals money from his kid's college account to buy a BMW with the belief that the car will make him happy. It does, for a while. Then, in a matter of weeks, it's just another car, and he's got a residue of guilt to live with. It's as complicated as the woman who avoids all involvement with men because she thinks she can't handle the feeling of being demolished when it's over. The truth is, she could handle it. The anxiety over the possibility rules her; to avoid the anxiety, she avoids any intimacy (which of course leaves her with another feeling, isolation, but one which she judges to be less intolerable than demolishment).

The Professor was in good shape, you see? I would guess that at the time of his expiration he was reliving the act of killing his wife, letting the motion of the knife zipping across her spinal cord flow into his final breath. What else could account for the look on his face?

THE LAST FEW words are blank on the page. You can see a faint imprint of the letter, but not the inked letter itself. I punch "O" several times; it strikes and falls back, fainter each time. The ribbon is twitching, but not moving. It's wound down. As I recall, the ribbon is supposed to reverse itself when this happens, so it starts winding in the other direction, and this keeps on until the ribbon is worn out. This ribbon looks fairly shot. I find a little switch close to the spool, and throw it, and type a few letters, and they are imprinting, but now in red, almost scarlet, bright and sharp. Fitting, I think, and leave the switch where it is.

I think back to when the girl and I walked down the aisle in the car to our seat, after the scene in the vestibule. The air was heavy, unmoving, glowing slightly. I watched her fingers brush the tops of the seats as she passed by and realized I couldn't remember touching them, in spite of all the other places I had touched. I imagined the signals transmitting from her brain down through her arms and wrists to her hands, telling them when to touch, when to untouch. Her slender, unpainted fingers had touched my face, my dick, herself, and now they floated onto seat tops only inches from unseeing, unknowing heads. I wondered if the perfume of them would seep into the dreams of the poor devils, light in their projectors strange and erotic, even scary images. I followed her carefully down the aisle, placing my hands just where hers had been. Perhaps now that sex was over we would separate and return to our seats and sleep alone the rest of the night through. Two or three in the morning, I thought. A long way yet to go, with her and the other lost souls on this night rocket. I watched her hips sway, but with a faint sadness at the loss of the intense desire I had for them moments ago. I placed a hand on her right hip and felt the movement of the bones as she shifted weight. She turned her head slightly in my direction, with a slight smile, as if in reassurance: I might not need you anymore, but I still like you.

THE SWING FROM power to weakness is immense, I think. From the primitive to the finished. We develop ways of dealing with la petite mort. The old cliché of having a cigarette. Talking your way through it. Telling the other person you love them. Leaving. The boy knew nothing of this; he was captivated by the feeling of loss and aloneness after such passion, and of course he thought it was peculiar to him, to them. He let his hand fall away and dropped back a step, then two, until he could see her complete form. She seemed more untouchable, more alien than when he had first laid eyes on her so long ago.

I WAS HIT by an intense wave of tiredness. Wobbling between the seats. Water, I thought. A paper cup of water, from the dispenser at the front of the car. I turned back. The conductor was standing at the door, arms folded, staring at me, at us. I lurched back into the darkness. She'll want to sleep, I thought. Spread out on the seat, with her coat as a pillow. That's that, I thought, with relief. You've got the story, she's got the story.

Then I saw her, sitting in my seat. With that mysterious half smile, eyes knowing something beyond what they're seeing. "I put your jacket up top," she said. She scooted over to the window seat, left her hand on the empty one.

THE BOY SEEMS so hapless, always thinking he knows what's coming next, always wrong, but hanging in there. A likeable kid, occasionally turning his head to see the shadow, but never quite fast enough. Thank God for the girl. That she happened to be there and she was who she was. It's this next part that is a little sketchy, what happens after I sit down. I know we stayed together, because I can see the faintest light of dawn pass over her face. Images have flitted in and out over the years, but never in a way I could hold onto, from one time to the next. Her hands clenched on her lap, a soft fluttery voice, caught in muted pain. Her lips parted for breath, eyes awash.

Between there and here is an emptiness and I can't move into it, not now. I hit the carriage bar and swing it back, and hit it a couple more times to move a few lines down the page. The red ink is startling. I read in the paper not long ago that my first wife had died. We hadn't seen much of each other since the wedding in Jamaica. Still, it was a shock—to see her name in black letters under a picture taken of her in her thirties, about the time of our split. "After a long illness," it said, which almost always meant cancer. She hadn't called to say good-bye, I remember thinking. We had some good years. Perhaps a note, or a word through a friend. I never blamed her for the divorce, or even for fucking David. The night I walked in on them I stood there and watched in silence, absorbing their heat. They didn't lose their rhythm until finally he moved around from behind her and spread her legs and buried his face in her. She raked her nails up his back as she came. I could have been angry, the double betrayal. But I wasn't. Not at either of them. What was I, then? Captivated by the images. Impressed at the audacity of it, their mutual skills and enthusiasm. Even when it was obvious it wasn't their first time I didn't get pissed. Beyond that, I don't recall feeling much of anything. A little sorry for her because David was a prick. She used to say to me, when we were married, that I was a black hole into which she could lose herself if she wasn't careful. "You're not there," she would say in frustration. "You seem like you are, but you're not." I argued, of course, told her that I cared for her, but without much conviction. How do you tell the person who has attached herself to you in the belief that you love her that you're with her because the idea of being truly alone is too scary?

That you're playing life in a way to avoid that feeling, and you try to do your best at pulling it off, even to the point of thinking the right thoughts you hope might get you there?

"What really pisses you off?" she would demand. "What really gets you? Makes you want to scream or hit somebody?"

"Nothing I can think of right now," I would say, if I said anything at all, and she would shake her head and mutter, "That's the fucking problem."

So, I would get pissed when she got home late from shopping and we missed our dinner reservations. She would look at me, trying to divine the sincerity of my anger, the dimensions of it, and I would do whatever I could to convince her, including calling her selfish and insensitive and not caring about me. I think now, looking back, that my pauses gave me away. They were in the wrong place. That pissed her off even more. At which point I could only shrug; what do you want? "You," she would say, "but there's no one there." It usually ended in tears, and I would try to comfort her, but that only seemed to make it worse. Which I think I understood at the time was probably the reason she put on the show with David in my bedroom. To see if she could get me to crack. It didn't work, of course. Like I said, I found myself captivated by the imagery, the smells and the sounds, the crashing of a lamp on the floor. I wasn't eroticized, as I know some men are by the thought, much less the sight, of other men fucking their wives. True, I felt the absence of feelings—you should be pissed—but even that seemed to bother me little. As for David? The one who had lured me into Willie's den? That's a little trickier. He was smiling at me as he pounded into my wife; he even gestured that I could take a turn if I wanted to. He was doing me a favor, his smirk said. I should be grateful to him, just as I should be thankful that he had led me into other adventures in life. He was taking care of things, as usual, getting me out of a marriage I really wasn't suited for. I did feel some sense of invasion, but it was nothing I could act on, and whatever it was it quickly evaporated.

The feeling-nothing syndrome, which I was so often invited to feel badly about by my first wife and others, I would now view through the lens of the Professor's theory on moral neutrality. Anger comes from the need to condemn one for violating yourself; love comes from the need to have someone make you feel not lonely. If you are nothing that you created, if you exist simply as one of the swaths of goldenrods along the edge of the country road, the sparrow singing in the tall sycamore outside the cottage window, you are always like the newborn who takes no responsibility for who he is or what he's to become. You judge no one. You experience every moment as equal to the other, for the pure joy of it, like drinking a good wine or, as in the case of the Professor taking a good life. You treasure it the way the tree treasures Buddha, the way a cat prizes the mouse, the rose the sun. You perceive it and let it go, to be what it will.

It occurs to me that if I were a little more like the Professor, I could, theoretically at least, embrace confusion as much as clarity, which would undermine the very thrust of this entire effort.

The girl on the train is of course the wrinkle. She doesn't easily fit within the view. I see now she's never disappeared; she has prevented me from sliding into neutral and viewing the experience of living from a transcendent state. She has held me together, really, the glue on the tiny sticks of a toy B-17. Or better, a single thread through the panoply of images and memories and insights and splintered thoughts that allow a quasi-self to form and function. In a manner of speaking, at least. I did care about teaching and writing. I enjoyed the students, elucidating theories of human motivation. But that was because the self I brought in there was not that different from the self that drew stick figures on the living room wall for art, the barely coagulated one. When the dean's people moved in, I was finished. And I was better for it, for it allowed me to walk away from things like the article on the wellspring of human nature. I really don't care if people gain any understanding of why they do what they do; most, in fact, prefer to remain ignorant. You have children out of instinct. You drink because you believe it will make you feel better. You get out of bed in the morning because you think you must have hope.

I understand that the girl—or perhaps the entire night on the train—has evolved into something approaching myth. What was real that night is still part of the story, but ever so much more has been colored in. I can sense her presence here with me now. The beauty in her sad, feeling eyes. The touch of her lovely fingers on mine. The ever-so-slightly plump lips. She's asking me something, waiting for my answer. As if there's something there for me to tell and she needs some help in unwrapping it. We've tasted each other, and with that, I'm beginning to realize, comes some sort of obligation, of exposure, or disclosure. I feel the tremendous pull of her eyes, which tells me something lies deep beneath them. Me for you. Us for them. The exotic look could easily unravel me. My eyes drop to her breasts, her waist, her bare, tightly closed knees. The experience of her is floating away. I don't know how to hold onto it. Her body is already far beyond the pale.

A loud clatter on the wooden floor startles me. An elongated object. I nudge it forward with my toe. The knife. It must have fallen from my lap, yet I have no memory of putting it there. I lean over and touch the knife. I pick it up by the handle, hold it straight out, let it fall. It sticks in the wood and shivers in a blur.

MY FIRST WIFE's obituary said she had remarried and had two children, two grandchildren, and owned a gallery in Des Moines. Services would be held in two days at a funeral parlor not far from my apartment. After some consideration, I decided to attend the viewing. We hadn't ended up badly, after all, and there had been some good times, although I doubted she would have attended my funeral. When I arrived, all the mourners were gathered in a far corner, on the opposite side of the room from the casket, a shiny gunmetal gray. She lay out in the coffin in a blue dress. Around her neck was a two-strand pearl necklace I had given her for a birthday. Her nails were a bright pink, and rings of diamonds encircled her left finger. Her face wore an unfamiliar look; uneasy, anxious almost. A form beside me said:

"She wanted to be buried in the necklace."

I turned: it was David, in a tailored blue suit and burgundy tie. He reached out and touched her hand, as if inviting me to do the same. I glanced at her husband across the way; a short, slightly pudgy man in a sports coat and slacks. We had met once before, in a restaurant. He was a neurosurgeon whom she met shortly after her affair with David ended and married within a matter of months.

"She loved you," David said. I turned back. The usual smirk was absent from his face.

The husband was looking at us. I touched her ice-cold wrist.

"She didn't want you to know she was dying," David said.

Why would she care? I wondered, but said nothing.

She loved me, David had said, as if we all understood the meaning of that word. She had an idea in her mind, which didn't pan out. Me? I was only trying the relationship on like a suit of clothes, to see if it could give me a bit of respectability, a bit of continuity. The place was getting thick with people, the air heavy with the humidity of perpetual sadness. Faces I almost recognized floated up and said something, then disappeared. I headed for the door. A touch on my shoulder stopped me.

It was her husband. He said my name. Reached in his pocket and pulled out a white envelope. On the front in large black letters was my name. "She left a note for you," he said, handing it to me. He started to say something else, "She . . . ," but touched his forehead with a hanky and left. I slipped the envelope in my pocket and walked out the door, down the red-carpeted hall past tall vases of artificial flowers and large, gold-framed paintings of angels floating in billowy clouds. Outside, I paused. I pulled the envelope out, studied the lettering—it was her handwriting—and held it up to the light, looking for what, I didn't know. A plastic toy. A joint. A photo, of us. I tossed it in an aluminum bucket stuffed with sand and butts. She wanted to say good-bye, but on her terms, a one-way conversation. She did it to make herself feel better, I thought, to unload something before the finality. Nothing good could come from reading it. Although there had been no recriminations or accusations at the end, I remember the gradual sinking of hope in her eyes, and it was killing me. I began the process of ending it. I stopped fucking her. I left early and stayed late at the college. On the weekends I read and drank. She was smart enough to see the plan, and she went along with it, a shared delusion that I had once been there but was leaving, or had left. That I had never been there was a truth better left unsaid. She was dying from lack of oxygen and needed out the door, and we conspired silently to make it as respectable an exit as possible. We went five days without speaking, two unleavened ghosts wandering alone in the same house. On the sixth day I awoke to an empty bed, an empty house. No note, no message on the machine. It was painful, yes, but feelings of relief flowed in like a rushing tide. I had never misled her, misrepresented who I was or what life would be like with me, I told myself. I never assured her that despite her doubts *I was really there*. True enough. But I didn't dispel the notion either. I never said, "You're falling for an empty box, a contrivance." Perhaps deep in the miasma lay the hope that she could provide the substance, the ground. If so, it was a stupid hope, a cruel hope.

Halfway across the parking lot I turned back to the parlor. I couldn't have someone else finding and reading the note, whatever it said. I pulled it from the sand, shook it out, and stuck it in my coat pocket. I skipped the ceremony at the cemetery.

That had been, what, a month ago? Two months? I still hadn't read the letter.

I LEAN OVER in the chair, hook the handle of the knife back with my forefinger, pull it back, and let it snap forward. The tip stays stuck in the wood as the handle whips and blurs.

As for David, he had caught me in the funeral parlor parking lot and invited me to his house for a drink. I declined, and he persisted, and I said I would think about it, and drove off. We hadn't talked of Willie since I went away to prep school. The myth of our friendship evaporated when I came to see him as a truly a selfish prick. Now, I wish I had gone, to study him like a bug stuck on a slide. I believe now David was trying to recruit me for Willie back then. He saw nothing wrong in it, like he saw nothing wrong in fucking my wife, and in fact no one is in a position to judge him for it. And perhaps screwing my wife was his way of getting even with me for bailing out of Willie's room, or showing me that in fact he liked pussy. Although why David cared what I thought I can't imagine. I admire him, really, for the blasé way in which he carries himself. The look of sincerity on his face when he said my ex-wife had loved me. He doesn't feel bad about anything he's done; he is without guilt or remorse. David is the Professor's prototype of the morally neutral actor. If he killed Willie, it was not an act of rage, an explosion, or even revenge for harm suffered. He did it because Willie's time was over. He accurately predicted that he would feel better for it, for clearing the stage of a no-longer-useful prop. David was simply acting out his lines, following the stage direction.

Feelings of betrayal and revenge are worthless feelings, are they not? They only serve to bring you low, to hide the beauty of the world from your sight.

I reach for the knife. It has sunk in deeper in the plank than I thought. I jerk it hard, back and forth. It flies from my grip and clatters across the room. Let it lie, I think. No more blood, for now. When I left the alley, where did I go? I only remember realizing that Willie's death made sense, but still there was an uneasy feeling of lack of completion. It must have been then that I decided to leave town and come up here to the lake in the north woods. But hadn't I taken Thesis to a friend's house earlier? I turn back to the typewriter, as if it held the answer to all the questions, which in fact it did.

I turn the knob on the roller, then turn it again, until the paper pops out and flutters off the edge of the table and onto the floor. I pick it up and lay it on the stack, which is now close to an inch. On the train that night, I didn't think much about who the girl was, or why she was doing what she was doing, until we were sitting in the train car after having sex in the vestibule and the sadness of the aftermath threatened to give way to an intimacy more intense and beguiling than when we were fucking. I sometimes lost track of her words, not just to the steady clickety-clack of the wheels, but in her eyes, which never left me, which seemed to be on the verge of consuming not only me but the entire rocket and all in it. She would catch herself, smile, sit back a little, and sigh. "Well," she would say, her eyes recovering, "tell me about you." I would tell her something unimportant, like I played first base on the baseball team, because I was left-handed, but that I couldn't hit, or that I had earned only two merit badges in Boy Scouts before being kicked out. She asked what for.

"Smoking."

Her blue eyes glistened in the lights of a passing town. "Luckies?" she asked.

I nodded.

She reached in the seat behind her, and her breasts turned with her shoulder, and suddenly I wanted desperately to touch them. Before my hand could even think of rising, she turned back with a smile and the pack of Luckies. She tapped the silver paper on her finger, until one slid out. She held it lightly between her fingers, ladylike.

"It needs to be packed," I said.

She handed me the Zippo. "Show me."

"You hold the cigarette loosely in one hand," I said, managing it between the thumb and forefinger. "Like this." She leaned a little closer. I dropped my hand, released the butt at the last second, it smacked the lighter, and I caught it expertly on the bounce. Then I whacked it again on the case, harder this time. Her breath caught, as if she were witnessing a high-wire walker, and I made the mistake of looking at her, and the butt slipped from my fingers and onto my lap. My cheeks flamed. How many hours had I spent perfecting that move? Four or five good whacks, while you were talking to someone or gazing nonchalantly across the room, and the weed was hard as a pencil, with a slight flare of paper on the other end to blaze up when you struck the fire. All in a few seconds, unless you purposely drew it out, lingering, with pauses, for effect.

The girl laughed, not unkindly, and plucked the weed from my
lap, brushing the tip of my dick in the process, a little more roughly
than was necessary. Her eyes were merry as she reached for the
Zippo. When she first whacked the weed on the lighter, it flew from
her fingers on the bounce, and I went to retrieve it from her lap,
perhaps to brush her breast, but she was too quick for me. By the
third try she caught it.

I reached for the weed and the Zippo. I whacked the weed two,
three times, each one harder than the one before, the sound now
like a muffled gunshot. I turned the end around to face her. She
touched it, then let her fingers slide down the length of it, and then
back up. I don't lust for you, I wanted to tell her; I just want to feel
your breasts without desire or need. Them and me. No you.

To avoid a feeling of loss, I realize now, with some clarity. A
foolish hope.

The Zippo was heavy in my hand, and she tapped it with her
nail, as if to say, "Now?"

THERE IS, AND was then, and always will be, an art to handling a Zippo. You hold the metal case with your three fingers
on the back edge and your thumb resting on the crack separating
the lid from the case. With one smooth motion, without looking, you brush the lid up with your thumb, and as it clinks open
you brush the same thumb down on the wheel. The flame shoots
up. Glancing to bring the tip of the smoke to the flame, you hold
the fire there just long enough for one short pull—if it had been
packed right, that was all you needed—and then you snap the lid

shut with your first finger. Clunk! And the lighter disappears into your pocket. As the smoke hits the back of your throat, you take the cigarette from your lips, drop it to your side, and exhale. Two seconds at most.

A few days after the detectives showed up at our house, my father gave me his Zippo for good. He was, in his own way, telling me it was OK. I would work it in my pocket. Clink-clunk, hard and clear, it rang out. I rubbed my thumb over the Marine Corps emblem until it grew shiny and almost smooth, except for the top of the anchor.

I carried the Zippo on my newspaper routes. In the bitter, dark winter mornings, on the corner where they dumped the bundle of papers, I would light it so I could see to untwist the wires and count the papers. I would slip in an apartment building to warm up and use the Zippo to light my first smoke of the day. At a party, the lighter appeared from nowhere, fired a woman's cigarette and disappeared before she knew it.

I had the moves down so smooth others were almost in awe: Flash up, clink, fire, clunk, flash down, gone. I carried the lighter for years. In every pair of slacks or jeans or shorts it lay hard against my thigh. Even after I quit smoking in graduate school I carried the Zippo.

One day the Zippo was gone. I missed it as you might a hand or a foot. I tried to replace it with a new one from Woolworth's, but it was smaller and didn't have the Marine Corps emblem and hadn't been carried over the bleeding lava of Tarawa. I can feel the Zippo in my hand now.

Moonlight is glancing off the shiny chrome case. In my favorite move, I position two fingers on top of the Zippo and the thumb on the bottom and snap my fingers. Clink! the lid flies open. I brush my thumb over the wheel and Whoosh! a dancing blue and yellow flame shoots up. I put a finger into the flame and pull it back. Clunk! The key, I remember now, was striking the wheel just right. If you hit it too hard, it would jam down on the flint and stick. If you didn't hit the wheel hard enough, it would spin over the flint. To have to strike it more than once was to fuck up. The flame needed to dance just high enough that you could cup your hand around it in the wind and lean in without scorching your eyebrows. I used to keep a can of lighter fluid in my desk, and every three days I would remove the casing from the lighter and squirt in enough fluid to dampen the absorbent cloth. The tiny red flints came in a little yellow plastic packet of six or seven, and I popped one out and into the Zippo every two weeks, whether it needed it or not.

I didn't show off to the girl on the train. After the weed was sufficiently tight, I simply flicked the top open, lit it with one pull, and closed it. Clunk. She took the lighter from my hand and snapped it open and struck the wheel, and a gold flame flickered in her eyes. She snapped it shut. She asked where I got it, and I told her the story of my father and what he did to the Japs on Iwo. She was silent when she handed the Zippo back to me, like it was a sacred relic, which it was.

Somebody must have stolen the lighter. I would never have left it anywhere. It was always either in my pants pocket or on top of my wallett on the dresser. I think back to the day I realized the

Zippo was missing. The first day of my honeymoon. My wife and I were eating breakfast on the deck of our cabin overlooking the water in a coastal village. I poured myself a cup of coffee from the percolator on a side table, slid a Marlboro from the pack, and reached for the Zippo, like I had a million times before. Gone. I patted all four pockets, in growing concern. My new wife thought it was funny at first, but not for long. I tore through all of my luggage, and then hers. Then the entire cabin and the rental car. The ground around the cabin, the stone path down to the dock where we had walked the evening before. The shallow waters.

On the day of the canoe trip across the lake I had left the Zippo in my jeans, hung over the chair in my room, the one halfway down the hall at the bottom of the stairs. I had found the lighter in the pocket when I returned to the house the night of the drowning; the night, I suddenly realize, I had almost drowned as well. The water had turned freezing, and the black wind was slapping crests of water into my face. I could not tell which way the shore was, but I paddled anyway, kicking and flapping my arms. My right leg cramped up, and I cried out. I tried to straighten the limb, which was now locked up against my chest. I lifted my head up and swallowed the cold lake water and began coughing. You might not sink down under the water and drown, I remember thinking, but you'll grow weak enough and drown from the water in your lungs if you can't get any air. Found floating face down with a life jacket on. I fought panic. Kicked my leg straight, kept my arms still, my face up. The pitch black suddenly turned to a dark gray. I had hit the edge of the squall. "Where the hell are you?" I yelled. I turned over on my back and floated. A scream sounded, and I turned over and saw a shadowy figure on the beach waving frantically. A girl.

Sally screamed her brother's name. I can hear it now, taut with anger and relief. "Joseph!" And she was walking into the lake toward me, I can still see her red bathing suit, raven hair now wild in the wind, reaching and crying. The life jacket must have given me away. (Who could forget Joseph's contemptuous flinging of it away?) And then the brown hair, not the straw-colored mess she was expecting. She called my name. She tugged on my life jacket, backing up, until my chin scraped up on the sand. "Where's Joseph?" she demanded. "Where's the canoe? Where's my brother?" I could only shake my head. She screamed for her father.

I am stunned by the clarity and detail of the images in the narrative. Her pale skin, panicky anger in her voice, the rough scraping of my chin on the sand. The ice cold of the water in my lungs. I feel a rush of pleasure; the plan so recently formed and implemented seems to be working. The time spent here with the girl on the train, reexperiencing that night, is stimulating the images of the past to coagulate and seep through the less-than-porous membranes into the present. But this scene has a different texture than some of the others, such as the one in which Shelley Duvall's head begins to wobble on her swan's neck. *More concrete.* I can smell the lake water, feel the cramp in my right leg. I am short of breath as I sit here now. My hand shakes like one of the oak leaves on the branches now tick-ticking against the window. I would suspect that such images are more likely to reflect something as it actually happened, and that therefore in my own way and time I am approaching reality, or at least clarity. In an attempt to move it forward, I return to the moment Sally called out for her father and I was trying, without success, to bring my knees up under me on the sand. The reel is stuck. I haven't any images of the last minute in the water with Joseph in any unblurred, stable form, ones that I could rely on and say that's the way it went down. I fled or I didn't. I left him to die or I didn't. Which is the point of it all. But I am getting closer, the images more trustworthy, I believe. I straighten my back, sit forward on the chair, roll my shoulders back, close my eyes, let my hands rise and float over the tiers of keys, and wait for the rest of the piece to play out in my head, and from there through my fingers and onto the letters, like a classical pianist.

MY MOTHER WRAPPED me in a beach towel and rubbed me from top to bottom. When I finally stopped shaking, she put me in a tub of hot water. Then she hustled me off to bed, tucked me in, and shut the door firmly behind her. The doorbell rang a short time later, and I heard the sound of male voices. The bedroom door opened and two deputies stood there in brown pants and shirts and gold stars on their chests. I told them what I remembered; the canoe tipped over in the storm, Joseph and I got separated. Joseph wasn't wearing a life jacket. I didn't actually see him disappear. Joseph had been steering. I couldn't remember the name of the girls, or the camp. The deputies left to continue the search, and as soon as the front door closed I got out of bed and went to the window and watched them get in their cars and drive off in the settling darkness, red lights flashing without sirens. It was then that I heard the motors of the boats on the lake. Peering, I could make two white lights a ways out on the water. Too late, I thought. He's gone.

I lifted my jeans from the back of the chair, slipped my hand in the left front pocket, and pulled out the Zippo. In the right pocket I found a crumpled half-empty pack of Luckies. I tugged a weed gently out of the pack, held both ends, and pulled it straight. I whacked it gently several times on the Zippo, put the firmer end in my mouth, and glanced out the window over the black water. Joseph and I used to smoke in the woods. He ate mints so his parents wouldn't smell it on his breath. He left lip marks on the end of the weed and coughed after every drag. He was always impressed with my handling of the Zippo, like when I snapped it shut in a way that left a dead stillness in the air.

I watched the lights of the boats heading in opposite directions. My hand with the Zippo tried a new move I had seen flashed by local hoods outside the town roller rink. You whip the Zippo down and across your thigh to pop the top open, and like lightning you whip it back up your thigh so the wheel rubs your jeans and strikes the flint. The flame magically comes to rest at the very tip of your weed. You snap it shut. (Clunk.) All without looking. It didn't light the first try, so I pressed the wheel down harder on my bare flesh, and then a third time even harder, until it caught fire. The smoke bit into my lungs, and my eyes watered. I pulled the chair up to the window and sat. I drew again, then released the smoke slowly in the direction of the lake. I tapped the weed on a tin ashtray on the window sill. The chugging of the boats faded into the distance.

I READ OVER the last few pages. It's the best version I've got, I think, and a hell of a lot more than when I sat down here a few hours ago and thought of Joseph for the first time in well over twenty years. The hole in the middle of the story will fill in eventually on its own, better if I don't stare at it. I could use a smoke now. After all these years. I notice the boy in the chair by the window doesn't seem to feel particularly guilty over what happened. You think he would, even if he hadn't done anything wrong. Survivor's guilt. But he sits and smokes and looks out the window, certainly feeling something, but I'm not sure what. Mindlessly, I pat my pocket for a pack of weeds. God, it would feel good, just to have one in my fingers, the crinkly feel of it between my lips. The whip-snapping of my hand and the lighter popping open in flame. Suddenly, I could feel it, I could hear it. I stood and patted myself down again. I grabbed the briefcase and rifled through it. Thank God I had lost it *after* my father died. It would have broken his heart. In a way, the war was the end of his life. He let go of whatever lay ahead of him, accepted with finality and without regret that it couldn't compete with what lay behind, and settled into a long, slow demise. The more demanding my mother became, the blander he got. He would pretend to acquiesce in her rages, but really—I could see—he didn't care. The only thing he insisted on was his Saturday-morning golf game. That Saturday morning, he was out the back door with his clubs on his shoulder seconds after the front door had closed behind the detectives, and before my mother could say anything. So, then it was the two of us. I sat in the chair and waited, willing to get it over with. But she went silent. Finally, I got up and headed out the back door and got my bike from the garage. I kicked the stand back, threw a leg over the bar, and headed out. In those days, I roamed all over town, from the highway on one edge to the railroad tracks and stockyards on the other. Even the back roads to the cemeteries and sewage-treatment plants and power stations and the water tank, and back down the main street, past the movie theater and ice cream parlors and barber shops. To the swimming pool, where I remembered going after the incident in Willie's room.

This day, the day of the detectives' visit, I parked my bike outside the pool, went inside, and picked up an old suit in the lost and found. I paid my dime, got a towel, and went in the locker room. The suit was several sizes too big. There was a mother and her three kids at the baby pool and two girls splashing and screaming in the big pool. I walked to the deep end, held my breath, and tumbled into the water. I sank to the bottom and grabbed the drain, and slowly let the bubbles out, and watched as they rose to the surface. I tried to imagine what it felt like to be trapped underneath, the pain, the panic, and to see if there was acceptance in the final moments. At the last second, before my lungs burst, I let go of the drain and shot to the surface. One arm swung out ahead and pulled through the water and my legs began kicking and I flattened out on top and my other arm swung out and pulled out and down and I felt the water rush over my face. I turned and opened my mouth and sucked in a lungful of air. To my right I heard the girls splashing and laughing, and I kicked harder and ripped my shoulder through the water and brought my hand up fiercely and reached out and pulled. Whatever happened that day began fading. I dropped my head into a turn and pressed my feet against the wall and shot out like an arrow.

I've been looking out the window as I type. Hitting the return bar without thinking. Mesmerized by the steady rhythm of the click-clicking of the keys. Suddenly, my fingers seem to forget where the keys are. They hover uncertainly over the keys. It was Mrs. Roberts in eighth-grade typing who insisted that you were not to look at your fingers or the keys while you typed. Look at the paper you were typing from, look at the door, the floor, anywhere but at your fingers. And so I'd always done it that way, until something apparently interrupted the flow of impulses from my brain to my fingers.

I stand and feel an ache in my legs. I've been here for hours, since those moments on the porch with the caretaker, in the dimming light. The drive up had been by habit, like typing, amazing because I myself had never driven here before. I was on the edge of town before I realized where I was heading. I made the turns without thinking. Came to a stop at the grocery store in the center of the tiny town and asked the elderly woman behind the counter where the caretaker lived. She gave me an odd look, like I was an unwelcome ghost from times past. But she said nothing. It didn't occur to me to buy any food or water, and now it's well into the blackest hours and I still feel no pangs of hunger. My mouth is dry. I hold my hands out in front of me, stretch my fingers wide. I had worn a wedding ring in my second marriage, although the absurdity of it was apparent to me, and to her as well, I think, from the very beginning. It was what you might call an "arrangement." It suited us for different reasons. Music was her life; every other need or drive was subsumed to the cello. Even in a movie, or a play, she was practicing or writing a piece in her head. So there was only a certain amount of her present at any one time. You can see the fit with me. To the best of my memory, we never said we loved each other. Neither of us wanted anything from the other, except to be present at predictable times. In the beginning, the lovemaking was frequent and wild, but with little genuine feeling, like good pornography. Our true intimacy was the unspoken belief that we were living honest lives without the artifice and deceit so necessary in most relationships. Neither of us cheated on the other, there was no need to. Nothing to run from, nothing to worry about losing. It was there, until it was no longer. It was our belief, I think, that without need we might experience a deeper form of freedom. It was our own form of a lie, of perhaps simply a shared delusion, I see now. It allowed us to live without fear, which is no different than living to avoid any feeling.

I SHAKE OUT my hands, drop them to my side. Physically, I was in excellent health. Lean as a lodgepole pine from forty years of almost daily swimming. A full head of graying hair. A sound heart and lungs. My interest in sex had faded some in the past several years, which makes me highly suspicious that there was in fact a woman in my bed this morning. A dream must have lingered a little longer than usual; splinters and flecks of past times formed something slightly new and different, which led me to believe it was real. There had been the wine glass, though, with what looked at one moment to have been a coral lip print on it, and there had been the newspaper with the story of Willie's murder. I had thought of calling the police department for information, or even the newspaper, but decided it was foolish to draw attention to myself. Who knows what the detectives had left in their files? My name. My juvenile mug shot, from my arrest for shoplifting. The detectives, my detectives, were far too old now to be working this case. I suspect they were behind Willie's conviction and imprisonment that I read about several years later. It mentioned a felony in the article, which I had slipped into my briefcase before leaving my apartment. Five to ten years, probably out in two or less. I did see one of the detectives again. I was giving a reading from *The Professor* at a bookstore downtown—the owner was a former student of mine—when I looked up from one of my favorite passages—the Professor addressing the jury after it imposed the death sentence on him and inviting the members to attend his execution—and was startled by a face in the second row. The scar had faded as the skin had crumpled over time, but you could still see it, the way he was holding his head. And the look in his eyes: time hadn't softened the intimation that he knew more about you than you did. He was wearing a replica of the cheap coat and tie, although now there was a little more bulk to him. He was almost bald. He caught me looking at him, and the barest of smiles crossed his face. It was a smile of encouragement, I wanted to believe, of admiration for having pulled it off, after all. I was rattled during the rest of the reading, and during the questions I could feel his eyes on me, watching my every gesture as if it might confirm what he knew, or perhaps discern any hint of guilt or shame over what had happened thirty or so years earlier. I worried that he was going to come up to me afterward and say something, or buy a book and stand in line. "To my favorite detective," I would write. But by the time I made it to the signing table, he was gone.

I REACH FOR the sky and feel the tightness in my shoulders. I bend over and touch my toes, the white tips of my Keds, and feel the rush to my head. I straighten up. The blood draining from my head leaves a red halo around the moon. The red against the white is startlingly beautiful, a fitting image of the night as it has gone and is yet to go. I unlatch the window again and push it open, first a few inches and then all the way. The night chill on the late September air has sharpened. I take a deep breath and feel the cold spread through my lungs and into my bloodstream and through my heart to my limbs. If I had walked through life like this, I think, I would have awakened to the missed dimensions. Your mind as clear as the night sky, with a point of light banishing concerns and fears and allowing an unblemished clarity of sight and feeling. Let the fangs of night's creatures pierce your flesh, let assaults and insults and murders and attempts pile up on you, let failures seek to define you; your vision would be microscopically clear through the depths of your soul and out through the farthest reaches of the universe. By accepting all emotions, you would be the captive of none. As sadness wraps its cloak around you, you pull it tighter, seeking the full warmth of its embrace. Love you cherish the way you might an ancient brandy, knowing that when it's finished the sense of loss will bring you some comfort. You fear nothing, because you see everything. You're one of those glass globes that spins in the sunlight—and reflects the light back into the universe, untouched and unaffected.

A shadow in the corner of my eye, a ruffling of a wing over my hair. My visitor is excited by the blood moon, I see. I lean out for a glimpse and spot a speck in the round light encircled in crimson. I slowly pull the window shut and turn back to the illuminated darkness.

I feel good, neither hunger nor thirst nor fatigue. But I know, from the rhythm of the night so far, if nothing else, that this epiphany, this feeling of acceptance and understanding, will not last. The euphoria is momentary; it will succumb readily to the next image that burbles its way into the clearing. Something from somewhere for some reason of its own will intrude and unsettle the peace. It always comes back to the story of the girl on the train, as it must.

I SLIPPED THE Zippo in my pants pocket. The weed was oddly unsatisfying. Stale, like cardboard. I blew the smoke against the window; it bounced off the glass and dissipated in the darkness. The girl watched me quietly. She extricated the pack from my shirt pocket and knocked a weed out. She thwacked it against the face of her watch several times. She put the weed between her lips and reached for my hand, which she held lightly by the wrist. She leaned forward until the burning end was a millimeter from hers. She brought the red glow closer, glancing at me through the smoke, and the two ends touched. She puffed once, twice, then the end of her weed flamed brightly. She leaned back. Then started coughing.

I laughed. "Amateur." Pulled deep into my lungs, and blew one then two then three perfect rings, which floated slowly, delicately past her face. She poked her finger through them, one by one. Smiling, she brought her cigarette up to her mouth.

"It's harder than it looks," I said.

"Show me."

"You make your mouth into an O, then push the smoke out with your tongue. Like this." I blew several rings; one encircled her right breast; the other veered away and bounced off her elbow.

The light seemed to shade a little from her face, her eyes faded. Like somebody had switched channels. She was there with me, but somewhere else, too.

The door hissed and snapped open. The conductor made his way down the aisle toward us. He stopped a few rows ahead, picked the ticket from the slot overhead, read it. "Toledo," he said. "Five minutes." No response. "Toledo," he repeated a little louder. Finally, he reached down and ruffled a shoulder. "Toledo," he said again. "Five minutes." A body stirred, sat up. "OK," a male voice blurted. Two arms shot up in the air, followed by a loud grunt. The conductor continued, stopping here and there to check tickets, found another Toledo passenger, across from us, a woman, who thanked him and clicked on her reading light. She glanced over at us. Old as my mother, with glasses hanging on a string around her neck, brownish hair loosely curled.

I can see her now. Narrow eyes a mixture of curiosity and concern. She could have made herself known to us and put a stop to it.

She scooched to the aisle seat. "Where are you kids going?" she asked pleasantly.

Neither of us responded. "Chicago?" she asked. She slipped her glasses up on her nose and glanced at her watch.

The girl leaned forward a little. "Yes," she said. "You?'

"Here, Toledo. Lived my whole life here. Raised a family. My husband died five years ago, and I live alone now. All of my kids moved on, to the West. Montana, California."

"That's too bad," the girl said.

"I see them once a year. I have one daughter who calls every Sunday. They didn't like their father very much. I taught second grade for thirty-five years."

The girl glanced at me. Raised her eyebrows. The woman flicked on the light over the aisle seat. It was like an operating room.

"My students were my real kids," the woman continued. "Didn't really need any of my own. Life would have been a lot simpler."

The woman sat back. I glanced down at the girl's breasts, to see if they changed shape when she leaned forward. I cupped one, felt the soft weight as it molded into my hand.

A true moment of random harmony for the boy, I think to myself.

WHEN I WROTE the essays on the philosophy of violence, I included a final piece on the notion of peak experiences, which I called the theory of random harmony. The theory is based on the statistical concept of chance. The underpinning is that there is no underlying scheme or order to the universe. We construct moral order, but there is really nothing there except randomly spinning molecules, bouncing aimlessly around, that will—and here is the key—on occasion line up purely by chance to construct or create a moment of pure harmony or beauty. It happens as a matter of statistics; you can't seek it out, you can't make it happen. Thus, Chopin and Gaudi are statistical emanations. They are bound to show up sooner or later. Psychologist Maslow allowed that each individual had two or three such experiences in a lifetime; where everything worked the way you always wanted it to; every piece slipped into place, and for an incredible moment, the sense of being fully awake cleared out every other feeling.

The theory is somewhat nihilistic in the sense that it denies the possibility of achieving a higher order; it denies good and evil, every theory of morality, things like karma and transcendence, peace through proximity to God. What an individual *can* do, however, is create an atmosphere that will lay the ground work for the moment of harmony, that will allow it to flower, to flow, to be realized to the fullest, when it does appear. Heads full of fear and anger and selfish desire and ego and regret or guilt are not good bedding grounds for the realization of a moment of random harmony. It could pass unnoticed, and probably does for most people, or be barely felt, and you will be the less for it, will miss one of life's rare genuine pleasures.

Now I believe that the entire night on the train with the girl was itself a great extended moment of harmony, and there has been nothing like it before or since, and it was nothing I had deserved or earned. If I had gotten on the train two cars from the end, rather than the very last car, nothing. One of the risks, of course, and I wrote little about this, is that you would want to stay in that moment, and when you realized you couldn't, you would descend into a well of despair.

The early lectures on the philosophy of violence were well received. The college appreciated the wide attention they brought. As they proceeded to man and nature, man as nature, essentially denying moral responsibility, the reactions grew quieter. Still, I received an offer from a prestigious university press to publish the talks in a book (which I declined). The theory of human motivation was presented as an invitation to people to try to understand why they did what they did, and as such stimulated much discussion and debate. That people acted in their own perceived self-interest was an established Darwinian fact.

There were quarrels with academics and religious leaders, of course, but they were well within bounds of reasonable discourse. The real trouble began later when I wrote *The Professor*, demonstrating the principles in actual form, albeit in the guise of a novel. Moments of random harmony, it seemed, were supposed to be ones of great insight and beauty, where you intuitively grasped the theory of relativity or dashed out *The Stranger*. That an experience of pure harmony could come from the taking of a life, from murder, was inconceivable. As crazy as the idea that Hitler could have been in a state of genuine rhapsody when he conceived of the Final Solution. That the Professor never renounced the pleasure that the deed brought him, that he seemed happy—more than happy, fulfilled—at the end of his life, as he wrote about so vividly in his memoir, was the problem; that he accepted the ultimate punishment as simply the last act in the play of his life, that he didn't experience pain or remorse, or fear, all the things that go with moral judgment, was the problem. He behaved true to his nature; his moment of harmony left him in peace, which was to others simply intolerable. Peace comes from noble acts, to kind and caring souls, one woman argued at a forum. To suggest that a man could justifiably feel good after killing his wife was heresy. She had, of course, missed the point. As calmly as possible, I plucked the word "justifiably" from her sentence. I laid it on the podium. "There is your problem," I said. The Professor didn't feel he was justified or not justified. You are making that judgment. He simply acted in harmony with the deepest source of his being. And thus, I would go on, while such a moment of harmony is effervescent and unmaintainable, it will, if fully experienced, leave lasting and beneficial effects on the individual. And so the Professor died a happy man. Why does this anger us so? Why cannot we accept it? I would ask the audience. That was when the accusations started, the requests by some faculty members to the dean that I undergo a mental health evaluation. I could have easily passed with flying colors, but I refused, because I didn't want some label like "mentally sound" placed on me.

I didn't leave the campus out of fear or weakness; I could have fought and probably stayed on, and if my nature were different I would have. But when I thought of the feelings I would be entitled to in victory—triumph, vindication, superiority—I felt sure they would not bring any true or lasting sense of satisfaction or pleasure. I would necessarily in the heat of battle have been drawn into characterizing others and their statements. You're wrong. I'm right. It would have been a step backward for me, and that feeling definitely would have been an unpleasant one. So I left on my own terms, in my own way, with full retirement and my integrity intact.

In the few years since, I've kept mainly to myself, except for an occasional appearance at a college forum, or being quoted in an article about the origins of violence after some ghastly crime. I have an occasional lunch with my few remaining friends on the faculty, and now and then I attempt a game of golf at the city course. I swim every morning. But gradually my outside world has grown smaller, as my inward world has intensified.

In this state, I've sought to accept all the circumstances of my life as they were, including the fact that my mind would never settle out into a lasting, stable narrative. The lack of linear progression, the constant susceptibility to intrusion by vivid images, was simply the way my mental neurology worked, it was who I was, and that should have been that. But the shadow created by the lack of understanding became darker and more distinct after I left the college. I think the time I spent with the Professor's memoir may have amplified the discomfort. The man pulled you all the way inside his mind and left you there. I watched him approach his end at peace and with an open heart. It became clear that peace for me would come only with clarity, or at least a version of events that would hold up from one day to the next. I came to believe, without acrimony or bitterness, that once I achieved that understanding there really would be nothing left to live for.

One needn't be angry or depressed to let go of this life. It could be a moment of random harmony itself, and yes, you could argue that in this night here and now I might be trying to create such a moment of harmony, which would not be random and therefore not possible. Perhaps. I don't claim consistency in thinking or the application of principles. But what have I to lose? Even without blessed clarity, Aurora will bring the dawn to this curvature of the earth.

I SEE FROM the new lines on the paper that I've been typing for some time now. Going on about my thinking, rather than the night on the train. I turn back to the task at hand. The girl, of course.

She had fallen quiet. Her exotic eyes had grown dark. Seconds expanded. I asked her if there was something the matter. If I'd done something wrong. She shook her head.

"I hate this time of year."

"Christmas."

"It's more than that," she said, turning to me. She hesitated, seemed to study me for a moment, then, "I want to tell you something."

I wonder now if the whole night had been about this. From the moment she invited me to sit by her to her touching my hand in the bitter cold on the rear platform of the train.

I FEEL A sharp pain in my calf. I stand and try to kick it out, but it cramps up tight. I cry out in pain. I press my palms on the table and lean forward, until my knee snaps back. I massage the muscles. I see now that the boy on the train is beginning to remember something about what happened that afternoon at the lake. He's being manipulated by the girl now, by her need, her breasts, and I suspect there's little good that will come from that. Except, perhaps, the very thing I've been seeking, the very reason I'm here.

JOY

SUDDENLY THE HOUSE shakes, the windows rattle, in what appears to be a violent windstorm. The treetops are bending and swaying. A shutter slaps the side of the house. Over the lake the sky is still clear, the moon pulsing its waves of light into the turbulence, pulling my blood to the surface. I turn to the back window overlooking the drive, the porch where the box left by Sally sits, and there I see the trees are unmoving, still as grass. I step to the window, and my left leg crumples beneath me. I fall to the floor, on my side, and shout a curse. My head has banged into the edge of the chair, knocking the briefcase onto the floor beside me. I lie still.

The boy on the train, I see, is in the thrall of the girl, her need to reveal something of herself.

A FEW WHITE flakes hit the window, slid sideways on the glass, and then a few more.

The girl looked at me full on, her eyes reflecting struggle, aloneness. She turned, pressed a finger into the window. "You won't like me," she said.

"Try me."

"I've never told anyone the whole story."

She closed her eyes as if to gather herself.

"Smoke?" I finally asked.

A faint smile appeared.

I pulled out the pack from my pocket and extricated a weed. I put it between my lips, and she fired up the Zippo and leaned in to light it. I passed her the weed. She held it in between her thumb and forefinger, like a boy, and puffed. Her eyes watered as she handed it back to me.

"Let it cool down a little between drags," I said.

People around us rustled and groaned in their sleep.

"Let's move to the back," she said, "where there's nobody else."

I nodded. I slipped the Luckies in my shirt pocket, glanced around for the Zippo. The girl stood, leaned over her seat, and took her purse and coat. She held the Zippo up for me to see, then slipped it in a side pocket of her skirt.

We passed the lady with the crying baby, and the old lady in the shawl who had swiped one of my Luckies, bent up in the seat without an apparent head. The last four rows were empty. The girl picked the second one from the back. She settled herself by the window, lay her coat over her lap.

I waited for her to speak. Time floated by.

I can hear her voice now, as she finally began to tell her story. Low, unwavering. She looks steadily at me, although I catch a moment of hesitation. I am caught in the sound and vision of her, barely able to hear the meaning in her words.

"I had a happy family, once," she began. "There was my brother, Alex, my mom and dad, two cats and a golden retriever, and me. We lived in a large house in a suburb outside Chicago."

She paused, rearranged her coat.

"My father was a lawyer. Weekday mornings we drove him to the commuter station, where he caught a train to Chicago, and then my mother drove us to school. She worked part-time as an interior decorator, but she was always there waiting for us at 3:15. Every

Sunday night we practiced in the living room for our annual spring concert on the grounds overlooking the lake. Dad played the piano, I played the cello, and Alex played the clarinet. My mother sang. It was the way we started the new week. There was a feeling in the house like we were all in this together.

"Now, I can see things. My father worked constantly, and when he was home he stayed a lot in his office, where we weren't allowed. He and Alex did things together, but I think Alex was closer to my mother. Still, we were happy. I dreamed of going to medical school, Alex wanted to be a pilot or a policeman. Our parents loved us. When I looked around at my friends' families, I felt blessed."

I felt it coming, yet I could not look away.

"Alex was a shy kid who wanted everyone to like him. He kept to himself a lot, but he had an incredible butterfly collection. He would bring it in my room and tell me stories about each one, where they came from, why they were this or that color or had a certain marking. He would hold them in the palm of his hand and blow to raise their wings as if they were flying.

"One day when we came out of school our dad's car was parked at the curb, where our mother's should have been. The back door was open, and our father was inside waiting. He didn't say a thing on the ride. At home, he took us in the den, sat us down, and told us that our mother had left. He didn't know where she had gone, but he didn't think she was coming back. He handed us letters, sealed, with our names written on the front in her writing.

"Alex threw his letter on the floor and ran to his room. I opened my envelope. Inside was a single page. My mother wrote that she was very sorry to have to tell us she was leaving. She loved us more than anything, but she didn't love my father anymore. One day we would understand. It would be better this way, if we went on with our lives, rather than being torn between two parents. She would love us to her last breath.

"Dad walked from the room. He let the dog and cats out, made himself a drink, and turned on the TV in the kitchen. I don't think he ever spoke of our mother again. Her clothes and things were taken away the next day. Even her jewelry. He got us to school every day, but mostly he stayed in his office with the door closed.

"Alex never read his letter. He insisted that our mother was coming back. Or that she would send for him."

I KEPT STONE silent. We haven't got to the crux of the matter yet, I saw. It would play out in her head by itself, without interruption. The girl glanced out the window. In the reflection her eyes were strangely cool. Beyond the glass were shapes and shadows.

I FLIP THE light on and begin clacking away on the Underwood. The story is laid out minutely in stained-glass panels. Tap tap click clack bing! My fingers dart over the keys. I move the ribbon back to black; the letters are slightly faded, which is fine, things are on the verge of getting away from me. A warning flutters on the edge of the screen.

THE GIRL TURNED back to me. "Months went by," she continued. "Our father barely spoke at all. I was the only one Alex would talk to. It got smothering. He slept on the floor by my bed, and he would pray out loud for our mother to come home. I would wake up to the sounds of him crying.

"One day two school counselors came to our house. They asked a bunch of questions. Alex wouldn't answer them. Three days later Dad hired a live-in nanny, who cooked, cleaned, and looked after us. Then one night almost a year after our mother left, my father announced at the dinner table that in the fall I would be going away to prep school in the East. I wasn't doing well; they had smaller classes. Dress codes. It was fine with me, actually. Anything was better than staying in that house. But poor Alex, this screwed him up even worse. He began screaming at me. One night after dinner, he set the papers on my father's desk on fire."

The train rocked back and forth, the soft lights dimmed, went out, then flickered back on.

"But I left for school anyway. I called home when I could, but Alex wouldn't talk to me. When I came home a few months later for Christmas, things had changed. The nanny had moved into our father's bedroom. Dad told us at dinner on Christmas Eve that the two of them were getting married in the spring. Alex spit a mouthful of food onto his plate."

The memory made her smile.

"Alex begged me not to go back to school. I told him I had to. Our mother had wanted us both to go away. There was a panic in his eyes. He still held out hope for her, I could tell.

"You know she's not ever coming back, I finally told him one morning. He shook his head, he knew she was. She's in love with another man, I said. That's why she left. It was in the letter she left for Dad. I hadn't meant to tell him, I just blurted it out. *Ever*, I repeated as he left the room crying.

"I went to Christmas parties with my friends. I bought new clothes. A boy picked me up at the door for a country club dance in his new car. Alex stopped talking to me. He refused to come downstairs Christmas morning. The day before I was to leave, he came in my room, while I was packing. He pleaded for me to stay.

"I have to go back, I said. It's the best thing for me.

"That night, he huddled on the foot of my bed. I could feel him shaking. You have to be brave, I told him. Go back to your own bed."

She laid her head back on the seat and closed her eyes.

"When I got to school the next night the headmistress was waiting for me at the front door of the main building. She took me into her office and handed me the phone on her desk. It was my father. Alex was dead, he said. He had hung himself in my closet with a belt. I was to catch a flight home the next morning."

The last panel of the scene is brightly lit. The boy is naked. His head is bent sideways, a black belt creasing deep into the flesh. His toes brush the floor. Behind the glasses his eyes are closed.

I force in a breath of air, exhale slowly. Flick the bar on the Underwood a couple of times. The boy cannot move until the girl releases him.

"I THINK THAT I always knew what he was going to do. I have nightmares about him calling out for me. I see butterflies everywhere."

SHE WANTS NOTHING from the boy sitting next to her on the train, no absolution, no forgiveness, no release. Just the sense of shared despair. She wants him to absorb the images of her dead brother.

I'VE GOT THE image. I'll have it forever. The scene has a terrible beauty to it. I stay locked on her dark face, on the borderless eyes that threaten to consume me. I dare not touch her. I dare not show anger at the unfairness of it, only that I'm still there, with her.

"I found his glasses on the floor. I kept them."

"They fell off when they unhooked him," I said. Hearing them clatter.

She knows then that I've seen, that her brother's death, the secret of it, is now part of both our stories.

The conductor walked slowly by, pausing at the seat ahead to peer out the window.

"The cigarette," the girl said, pointing at my hands, amused.

I looked down at the weed, now burned down almost to my fingers. I twitched, and the ash fell on my pants. I stubbed it out in the metal ashtray in the back of the seat ahead of me.

The train wheels screeched and the whistle blew two long blasts. The train slowed hard, like it had run into a great wall of water.

"We're coming to a town," I said.

I looked away from her eyes, out the window, at a string of yellow streetlights and cars parked in front of small stucco houses. Boxcars rattled by. In the flash of the station lights I could make them out: Union Pacific. Southern Pacific. Burlington. Great Northern.

The girl believes she's not alone anymore. Her posture has changed. She looks at me differently, not as a lover but as a participant in her life. We sat quietly.

"Have you ever lost anyone close?" the girl asked after some time had passed.

The boy felt as if something was loosening up inside him, crumbling like an ancient stone wall on the edge of the sea. The silence settled around them until the images of her story began to dim. He saw the black squall in the blue sky.

"Not anyone close."

"A friend?"

He nodded.

"Can you tell me?"

"I'm not sure I know the whole story."

"There's a beginning."

I hesitated. Finally, realizing that if I did not tell her about the afternoon on the lake, about Joseph, we would part strangers, I began. I told her of that summer afternoon at the lake, how all the kids met up at the river to swim and play on the swing. I even told her of my crush on Sally. She smiled at that. I felt myself moving into the flow of the day, with the hot sun and the blue sky and the roughhousing on the riverbank.

"Joseph wanted to canoe across the lake to a girls' camp. We had done it the week before and met these two girls. I didn't want to go that day. Storms came up in the afternoon.

"But he talked me into going," I continued. "He shamed me. We left after lunch, when the water was calm. Joseph steered from the backseat.

"He wouldn't wear a life jacket," I continued. "I handed him one, but he laughed and tossed it away."

Her eyes grew serious.

"I almost got out. I remembered turning back to the river and tugging open the snaps on the jacket. 'Hey,' he called loud enough for everyone to hear, 'the girls are waiting for us.' He had me cornered."

The train jerked, slowed further. The clickety-clack was like a metronome. I had lost my train of thought.

I described the ride over: The water was calm, the sky clear. I paddled hard, digging for the deep strokes to match Joseph's and keep the canoe straight. You could see the beach a ways before we got to the camp. The canoes were all tied up. Only the two girls. The pretty one waving, the redhead watching, hands at her sides.

Several overhead lights snapped on around us. People were getting off here. The conductor came by, muttering the name of some small town.

I told her how Joseph and the pretty girl, whose name I couldn't remember, walked down a path on the edge of the lake hand in hand with a picnic basket. And how I was getting nervous as the time passed and they didn't return. I could feel a charge in the air, an intense unsettling, although there was still no wind and the sun shone brightly.

The conductor stopped in the aisle. He stuck two stubs in the clip over our seat. A tiny smile crossed his face as he moved away. The train crept to a stop. Slid forward a few feet, then slammed still.

There is a vibration in the floorboards. I push myself up to a sitting position and listen. It's the same sound I first noticed. The rattling of a child's toy and then a faint scraping. I touch my hand to my forehead, expecting a spot of blood, but feel only a slight bump. The cramp in my leg is gone. I need to get back to the story. I force myself to stand and regain my seat at the table. I type up to where I am.

I TOLD HER about Joseph and the pretty girl coming back from their "picnic" all smiles and rumpled up. How I tried to convince Joseph to let me call my father to come pick us up. He would have none of it, and the girl added it would get everyone in trouble.

"We were standing there, when I noticed a dark cloud forming about halfway out. A black dot in a blue sky. Right before our eyes it grew larger."

As IF IT were pulling the rest of the sky into it, I think. I rub the goose bumps on my arms. Tap, tap. Clickety-clack. My fingers are disembodied. I read what they write as a stranger. I twist the roller, and the paper falls out onto the floor. I wanted to crawl out the window and stand on the edge of the roof to pee, but feared the wind would swipe me off.

"It looked like a huge cloud of mosquitoes over the water," I type.

"When Joseph suggested I take the backseat, I figured he must really be tired, and that maybe he would hang it up when I declined. It only seemed to energize him more. 'Hell,' he said, 'I'll paddle back alone if I have to.'

"I grabbed a paddle and held it up to the sky. The storm was wider than the blade now and directly in our path. I pointed to the black smudge in the sky one final time. Joseph was kissing the girl now, and her hand rested on his shoulder.

"I got in the canoe and dug my paddle into the water. Joseph jumped in."

I glanced out the window: "Belmont," the sign on the station said. Never heard of the place. "All aboard!" the conductor called.

The train slid smoothly forward, swayed gently from side to side. Gave a short blast, settled in, and rolled on.

"The darkness was spreading over the water. You could see tiny whitecaps forming."

The girl had fallen quiet; the image of the water seemed to reflect in the luminosity of her eyes. The train seemed perfectly balanced on a cushion of air.

I describe how the wind hit us suddenly and lashed water in our faces. It caught my arms, the edge of the paddle. I looked back at Joseph; he was leaning forward, head down, eyes shut. The front of the canoe swung against his stroke, and I turned back and dug in.

The wind had now caught the tip of the canoe and was pushing us sideways. I dug harder and harder and slowly we straightened out. The rain came. First in sheets of nails, then in waves. I saw a tinge of fear in Joseph's eyes.

"His hair was plastered to his face."

I continued. "I saw that we had taken on a couple of inches of water. The sky was pitch-black overhead, the wind whirling this way, then jerking that way. I felt my arms weakening as we fought for every foot of headway. The canoe tipped to the left, and we almost flipped the other way trying to right it.

"Then the wind caught the canoe and turned it sideways into the waves. We rolled over in a flash. I flew out of the canoe, grasping my paddle. I felt a bang on my head and saw black."

I AM SURPRISED at the boy. How much detail he recalls and how calmly he tells the girl about the storm. He is watching the story play out in her eyes. The words tumble out of him before the thoughts form in his head, and the images are in Technicolor. He didn't notice her hands as they brushed the hair back from her neck, and she leaned in a little closer.

I STUDY THE sky for the slightest hint of gray around the edges, but it is still black as ink. I wind another piece of paper into the typewriter, flex my fingers. I feel the chaos of the storm now, see it in the girl's eyes.

"THE WATER WAS icy cold," I told her. "I took in a mouthful of water, and as I coughed I took in more water. I started to panic.

"Joseph was calling to me, but I couldn't see him. I saw the bow of the canoe in the top of a wave. He was hanging onto it by his fingertips.

"He kept screaming my name, each time a little weaker, more desperate. He appeared and disappeared in the water like a pink dot. The cold rain stung like bees.

"All of a sudden, Joseph appeared a few feet away," I said. "He had to tilt his head back to keep his mouth out of the water. He knew he was drowning. He came at me. He was going to grab me and pull me under with him. I felt a hand on my shoulder. I tilted under. I grabbed the hand. His head popped up and he tried to say my name, but only spit out water.

I paused, remembering it clearly now.

"I felt his hands on my leg. Grabbing at me, reaching up for my vest."

A sheet of lightning broke with a crack outside the window. The girl's face was ghostly white. Only the images played on in her eyes.

"I reached down for his hand. It slipped away."

I couldn't see beyond this. I was cold, and my eyes were out of focus.

Another sheet cracked over the broad plains. Trees and cars and farmhouses and even animals froze in the flash.

"His hand slipped off my foot."

The train seemed to settle down on the tracks, grip them tightly and shoot forward with a newfound determination.

"I reached for him again. I lifted my head from the water and gasped for air. Took two deep breaths and dropped down again, feeling for him. I swung my legs slowly about for him to grab."

I shivered. "I could have gone after him. I could have taken my vest off and dove down."

"You would have drowned," she cried.

I could see the end in her eyes. The squall still blowing on the edges, the leftover waves just strong enough to push the bodies to shore, up against the rocks, half a mile apart.

Sally was bending over the boy as he lay on the beach, crumpled.

"Where's Joseph?" she demanded. "Where's my brother?"

I saw the force of blame in her eyes. "Where's Joseph?" was the screech of a mad raven.

I waited as the boy in the girl's eyes tried to answer.

"I don't know," he finally croaked. He didn't know, of course, but he suspected. The touch on his ankle had been the last grasp of a dead boy.

The girl leaned in a little.

"Sally understood then that Joseph was still out in the water. She froze for an instant, then began tugging at my vest, as if she might somehow use it to save her brother. She took a few steps into the water, called out her brother's name. I rolled over on my back, lifted my head, and watched as she went further in. I struggled to my knees.

"She cried out his name again. The water was up to her waist. Her hands were at her sides. I went in after her. She was up to her shoulders when I reached her, still shouting her brother's name. I reached around her chin and pulled her back. Her head went under, her scream stopped. I leaned back into the water and stroked and kicked, until we slid up on the sand. She didn't move. I pumped on her chest; she rolled over and coughed out water. She looked back into the black water. 'He's gone,' I told her.

"She jerked her hands free and began pounding on my chest."

I PRESS MY palms to my eyes. The boy hadn't seen it then. Without her brother, Sally didn't want to live. Life without him would be unbearable. The feeling of the loss of him would leave her alone and in endless pain. She had never left town. Never left her brother. Never married, nor had children. Her posture when she stood outside the car was stiff and unforgiving; she walked with her head down as if there was nothing to see.

I can only accept the scene just played out as the way it happened. I believe that it is immutably etched in the eyes of the girl on the train. I pull in a deep breath, and tears accompany its exhale. The boy did what he could for Joseph without sacrificing himself. His mistake was in saving Sally from her desire to join her brother; she knew what lay ahead of her and she was entitled to avoid it. I see it now, but the boy could not have known it then. He misread the girl's damnation. He lived away not from the curse of taking a life but from saving one. He grew into manhood without the images of the story in his mind, only the harsh glance of Sally at the gathering the next day. Whatever self-judgment lurked in his being is now purged. He owes it to the girl on the train, he owes everything to her. There is no judgment in life. Only acceptance.

I FINISH TYPING the scene, reach out and flick off the lamp. The room blackens and is slowly illuminated by the light of the moon, which now hangs high and bright in the sky like a celestial ornament. I stand and walk to the window. I look past the moon into the stars. Another story for the universe to absorb, I think. The orb spins slightly to the left, and then rights itself. The rattling sounds, but far off, as if something has scurried into the bowels of the old house. Perhaps Sally is waiting outside the door, or at the garden wall, having divined my purpose and wanting to witness it. I would kiss her, if I could. See if there isn't the faintest spark of life in her.

The boy and the girl, I notice, have fallen silent. The metal-on-metal clickety-clacking is so loud, the train is moving so fast, yet the two of them seem to have found some sort of peace together. The images of his story fade from her eyes. They grow shallow, like the water at the edge of a calm sea.

THE LIGHTS IN the car flash on. The old woman in the shawl and the conductor are looking between and under seats for something she's lost. Complaints arise from a few sleepers. The conductor finally locates an earring hooked in her shawl. The lights dim.

THE BOY FOUND himself in growing discomfort, as if something was pushing up against his throat. The relief from having told the story of Joseph is leaving him. The wall has been breached, something else waits to be told. The girl is leaning forward slightly. Her eyes have left his story behind and have a gentle light in them. She holds out her hand to him. In it lies the Zippo. She turns it over, to show the barely visible engraving of my father's initials. R.L.M. U.S.M.C.

"It's so lovely," she says. "Don't ever lose it." She places the lighter on my palm. Her fingers linger on the globe and anchor, and then drop away.

I STAND AND walk over to the chair on which my coat is hanging. I lift it up and feel an unnatural weight. I swing it back and forth. I put one arm through it, and then the other; I straighten the coat over my shoulders. I was wearing it earlier today, at the alley where Willie was gutted. And on the drive up here. And wherever in between, still a mystery, and the solving of it, I see, is becoming more and more wound into the scenes of the past. I pat the side pockets. My left hand knocks something. Jesus. I tap it again. Perhaps I bought another one. A replica. I smile; I will toss it down the stairs to see what it scares up; or I could fling it out the window through the leaves at the moon, now dimming somewhat. I feel the ground shift under me, like the rocking of the train back and forth. The girl's face is smiling, as if with secret knowledge. Slowly I slip my fingers into the left pocket and brush hard metal. I know from the feel, the weight, that it is one of the original Zippos, the one that outlines itself in white on your jeans pocket. My thumb brushes the globe. It can't be. I pull it from the pocket and walk to the window. The globe is worn almost smooth. I open the window, and just before winding up to toss it I turn it over to see if the owner left his initials. He did: R.L.M. My hand drops to my side. The Zippo slides to the tips of my fingers. A flutter of wings in the air above my head, a shadow diving over the glowing object, arcing off through the wooden frame. The sound of the metal hitting the floor echoes. How did the girl on the train know where it was? I reach down and touch it; the globe and anchor glow red like embers. I grasp the edges of it, stand. My breathing has grown shallow, but my eyes, sharp as a sparrow's, spot the dent on the corner, from the time I had accidentally dropped it from a second-story school window. It couldn't have been in my pocket all of these years. I hold it up, turn it about in the light.

My thumb snaps the top up—clink!—and brushes down over the wheel—whoosh!—an orange flame leaps high and twirls like a manic dervish. Clunk! Perfectly executed. My hand flashes down over my jeans and whips back up with a flame. The fire dances blue and gold; in it I see a face of pain and a feeling of joy, even glory. I snap the Zippo shut and drop it in my pocket. The ecstasy of the moment will, I believe, lead the way to the terribly elusive clarity I seek.

I settle down in front of the Underwood. I leave the light off. My fingers settle over the keys, my eyes remain on the golden orb, now only inches from the window.

Yes, the cat with the tips of its whiskers flecked with Willie's blood. Jade eyes, stepping back slowly. I tap it out, without watching my fingers, like Mrs. Roberts taught us. The feeling I had then, in the alley, was one of—what?—relief? Purpose? Newly found. Understanding, possibly, as to what must have happened. I turn away, the image torched into the visual neurons in my brain, but feeling incomplete: I want to imagine the story of Willie's demise. I need to see it, not out of bitterness, but because I feel entitled to it, and to slip another piece into the ongoing puzzle of my life. I cast a final glance at the black cat, sitting back on his haunches, who was likewise casting a final glance at me.

I DROVE FROM there to David's house, a large structure built into the bluffs overlooking the Iowa River. I knew he had become moderately wealthy from expanding his father's printing business into nearby towns. He showed up occasionally in the paper's society columns. Thick hair now gray, a lock still falling over his forehead. Unable or unwilling to erase the sly smirk from his face. Other than my first wife's funeral, I had run into him only once in this small town since his wedding, and that was at a cocktail party at the president of the college's mansion, a few years before *The Professor* was published and I was still considered a leading light on the faculty because of my papers on human motivation. David had of course clapped me on the shoulder and said we must get together to "talk about old times." Even then, before my theory of moral neutrality had fully matured, I felt little animosity or bitterness toward my old friend.

I think curiosity was the reason I drove up to David's house late this morning. Had he killed Willie? What did killing him feel like? *How exactly* had he killed him? I fully intended to do nothing about it; there was no particular value to Willie's life, and David was simply acting out a scene in the play of his life, which he had not authored, as had none of us ours. So it was in a moment of relative ease and transcendence that I turned into David's drive: I

wanted only to understand what had happened, to hear the story
of it, and, yes, perhaps to some degree to experience the act of it.
I saw myself as neither cheerleader nor judge, only the interested
observer.

As I wheeled around the long curve of the sweeping drive, I saw
a figure standing in the open door of a large brick garage. Hands
hooked in his jeans' belt loops, one hip slightly cocked. He watched
in amusement as I pulled to a stop.

I stepped out.

"Good to see you," he said, holding out a hand.

"Likewise."

"How long's it been?" he asked.

"Since the funeral," I said.

"You still got the Chevy?" he asked, glancing at my rental car.

"Same one," I said.

"I drove it at your wedding," he said. "From the church to the
reception."

"I remember."

That image stopped us cold for a few seconds.

"Come on inside," he said.

"I just stopped by . . ."

"You read about Willie's gruesome end."

He turned up the walk and opened the door. It was as if Willie
were a mutual friend, I thought. It had been over forty years since
that day. Inside the house, a massive picture window scanned five
miles up and down the river and from his lawn to the clouds in the
sky. Leather couches and chairs, with a heavy Mediterranean feel.

A large Oriental rug lay over gleaming oak floors. On the coffee table I noticed a gold cigarette box with his initials on top, and next to it a gold table lighter. David offered me a drink, and when I passed he stepped into the kitchen and returned with a bottle of beer. He walked to the window. Pointed across the river. "There's our old neighborhood," he said. "The repair shop. Our houses. All still there." Judy Pauling? My mind went: Is she still there? And the postman? I saw David's approach—get to the heart of things right away, show there's no guilt, even regret over whatever had gone on forty years ago, or yesterday. I could have predicted it; whichever way the world turned, it never got the best of the guy. He would be smirking the moment they slid his body into the furnace.

"Do you think much about those times?" he asked.

"Now and then," I said. "I remember smoking on the steps behind the repair shop. I remember Willie."

His eyes stopped to read me, search for a hint of dissonance, blame, regret, anything that could be a threat.

"He lived a long, full life," he said.

I laughed. David's cool cracked for a moment.

"Funny?"

"Willie leading a full life," I said.

David lifted the beer to his mouth.

"How did he die?" I asked.

"The paper said he was stabbed to death in an alley."

"That's it?"

"What does that mean?"

"You know everything in this town," I said. "Who was it?"

His eyes grew hooded, brushing off the smirk.

"Why do you want to know?"

"Just curious."

He sat down on the couch. He reached for the gold box, flipped open the top, and offered me a cigarette. When I waved it off, he lifted a cigarette from the case. Pall Mall. Extra Tall. He fired the lighter, touched it to the tip.

"Remember these?"

"I smoked Luckies."

"LSMFT." The smirk was back. "Lucky Strike means fine tobacco." He smiled benevolently. "We did a lot of shit together in those days."

"A lot," I said. "Not all of it cool."

"We were twelve, thirteen," he said. "We got over it. You got over it. Look at you—college professor, famous author. I read your book *The Professor*, by the way. I loved it."

"Why would you kill him after all these years?"

He took a slow drag, eyes on me. "Man, you go right at it, don't you?"

THAT DOESN'T SEEM quite right. The scene is missing something. It's moving too fast. There was an odd feeling of living in the past. I felt my old attraction for him: the cool guy with his dark hair swirled back into a ducktail, who always knew what was going on. I remember resisting an urge to let go of the whole Willie thing. I think it went more like this:

"I read your book *The Professor*, by the way. It's perfect."

"Really? It doesn't seem like your sort of book."

"Hey, man, he had it right. If the Professor felt he was entitled to kill his wife for fucking his neighbor, then he was. We're all animals, you know? We do what we think is right."

"Did you read his memoir, *The Joy of Killing*?"

He nodded his head. "The way I see it, you're the Professor. The picture on the back should have been you."

Really? I thought, but said nothing. The smirk reminded me of the old days, when he always had the upper hand.

"Well," he picked up, "I loved the way the Professor handled those assholes who called him names like psychopath or sociopath. The more they saw he wasn't bothered by what he did, the more pissed they got. He never felt bad about anything. He went to his death a happy man. I admire that."

I let that sit there. Seconds passed.

"Are you a happy man?" I asked.

That seemed to startle him. I sat down in the chair opposite him.

"Why do you ask?"

"I was thinking about Willie."

"I don't think Willie was happy."

"I mean about what happened to him. Why it happened."

He took a long pull on the Pall Mall, let half the smoke out, pulled it in through his nose, and let it drift out of his mouth in a gentle stream. I half expected him to spit on the floor.

"You think I killed Willie?"

I shrugged my shoulders.

He studied me carefully through the haze.

"I figure that over time the stuff between you and him got to be more than you could handle, and at some point you realized the only way to reduce the feelings was to kill him."

"Like the Professor," he said.

"Kind of. It would erase a lot of bad memories, balance things out. Leave you free and clear. Happy, in other words."

"Even if I admitted it, no one would believe you."

"Why would I tell anyone?"

He gazed out the window for a second.

"Maybe you've got a grudge against me, from the old days."

I figured he would be worried about this. But, truthfully? I would have told him that whatever happened that day, years ago, I owed him no ill will. "No one wrote their own script" was a favorite line of the Professor's, and I believed it. As for my wife, that never did bother me. I was in neutral on both counts. I was in neutral, period.

"Like you said, we were kids. As for my wife, you got both of us out of a bad situation."

David thought about that for a second, then stubbed out his cigarette in a black marble ashtray on the end table. He stood up and walked to the window. Turned back to me.

"It had to be done," he said in a calm, almost flat voice. "Willie wanted money. He had photographs of me, from a long time ago, no one would have cared about anyway. It was just time. He needed to be gone."

"I get it, but why the alley? Why the knife?"

David took a step back; now I could barely make out his features.

"He wanted to come up here, and I couldn't have that. I suggested the tavern. I got there a few minutes early and waited in the alley next to it."

"How did you do it?"

"How?" He came forward, toward the table, stopping only a few feet away. I kept my seat. He turned to the counter and picked up an ebony-handled hunting knife with a viciously curved blade. His voice took on a harsh timbre. "With this. I heard him shuffling down the sidewalk with his cane. I let him pass by and then grabbed him from behind."

David's arm hooked out about neck high.

"I pulled him back into the alley. He didn't struggle, didn't make a noise. 'Willie,' I said into his ear. 'It's me, David.' The cane fell from his hand. All he could say was, 'I know.'"

My host's grip tightened the knife to his quarry's neck.

"I sunk the tip of the knife in the base of his throat and pulled up. I felt him begin to slip, and I held steady, and he fell against the knife which ripped up his throat and into his mouth. He was hanging there, his jawbone hooked on the blade, twitching. I jerked up once or twice, felt him loosen. I turned him around, watched the light in his eyes fade, and jerked the knife back out."

David was standing over the body, crumpled on the alley floor, with the blood-dripping knife in his hand. He was breathing hard. He looked up at me.

"You looked like . . . you enjoyed it," I said.

His eyes were bright. "It felt good. Things were straight. I felt nothing toward him, only release in myself." He carefully laid the hunting knife on the table.

I could see the blood on his hands and shoes, hear the throttled croak of the lump on the floor. The crazily bemused look in David's eye was disturbing. I stood up and told him I needed to use the bathroom. He looked somewhat amazed, like after all that, the beauty of all that, and all you can think of is you have to take a piss?

I DROP MY hands to my lap. That's pretty accurate, best as I can remember. Some of the dialogue might be a little off. Hard to think it was only a short time ago. My throat is dry. I need water to make it through the next few hours. I'm reluctant to break the spell. As for Willie's death, it's as I thought; it seemed to have a certain harmony to it, the way it came about. That's not the end of the scene, though. The quiver in my chest tells me that.

"USE THE ONE in the bedroom," David said, motioning. "The one in the hall is torn up. Workers should have been here by now."

The bedroom is the size of my apartment. A four-poster bed of a mahogany frame covered by a silk canopy sits in the middle. Turkish rugs are scattered about. A small crystal chandelier hangs over a leather recliner and ottoman by the window. I pause. Walk by a wall of framed photographs on the way to the bathroom in the far corner. Just before I turn, I spot a picture on top of a heavy wood dresser. It looks like David, but without the lock of hair. His father. There is a flash of silver in the corner of my eye as it passes over the cluttered dresser top. Shiny. Flat, oblong. My eyes swing back to it. My feet freeze on the floor. I study the object in the mirror, from the back. A Zippo. *The* Zippo. I force air into my lungs, and it seems to activate a pulsing, gathering rage. *The bastard stole it from me.* He's had it all these years, sitting here on his dresser, in a ceramic ashtray, along with his gold cufflinks and money clip. I reach for it slowly, as if I'm afraid it might crumble in my touch. My finger brushes the dent on the top corner, then my fingers grasp the metal and hold the object upright. The globe and anchor shine brightly. I needn't turn it over, but I do. All these years, it could have been in my pocket; all the clinks and clunks it could have made. The reassuring touch on my thigh when I walked. I can see it sitting upright on the desk in my office, the sole symbol of sanity in my life, over the years. I feel empty from the life I've lived without it. There were the initials, just as I knew. R.L.M.

The metal grows heavy and hot. I bring it in closer, consumed by the sensation of it in my fingers, when I hear a voice behind me.

"I was going to give it to you," a face in the mirror says. I knew you would come up here after Willie."

David's eyes follow my hand as it drops to my side.

"I was always going to give it back."

He was trying to manage a smirk, and it contorted his features. I grasp the Zippo tightly, then relax, then tighten. My mind is racing back to the last time I saw it.

"The church," I say. "My wedding." The robing room in the church. I'm putting my tuxedo on, and my best man convinces me that the Zippo would look awkward in the tailored trousers. He appears to slip it into my jeans pocket, pats me on the shoulder, urges me to hurry up, we're behind time. The scene had completely dropped out.

"It never seemed the right time," he said, the twisted smirk now replaced by a look of some concern.

I slipped the Zippo in my pocket, felt the familiar heavy heat on my thigh. I felt strength from it.

"You don't mind if I take it now?"

He tried a nervous smile. "No, fuck no, man, it's yours. I feel really bad about it."

I take a step toward him, he tenses, steps back.

"I've got to go," I say.

"Hey," he says. "We're all right?"

"It was a long time ago."

"Good to see you."

"Whatever happened to Judy Pauling?" I ask, as he moves aside and I angle toward the door. I pause and await his response.

He looks at me nervously. "She teaches at Irving Elementary."

I smiled. "By the way, I brought something for you. A signed copy of *The Joy of Killing*. It's in the car."

"That's OK, man."

"You should have a signed copy. You and he . . ."

"That's all right," he said.

I reached for the door handle, twisted it, and stepped out onto the porch.

WHAT STRIKES ME here, as I lay out the scene, is how clearly and cleanly everything is flowing. The protagonist is reflecting very little on what he's seen or found, or what he's going to do about it. He's moving with clarity and an easy sense of purpose. There is no doubt or hesitation; he knows what to do, and he's going to do it. He is not ruffled or hysterical, or red-faced, or laced with anger or a need for revenge or payback. Impressive. Doing what comes natural, as they say. As for David, you can see the relief on his face. He's never known his friend as a violent man, although he did wonder somewhat after reading his books. He has considerable hope that his friend will just drive off. He still has the aftermath of killing Willie to deal with.

WALKING TO THE car, I felt the cool heat of a Midwest autumn breeze on my forehead. The leaf-covered stream twisting through the grounds has caught the light through the trees. You could ride a bike over the gentle hills of Iowa for hours on a day like this and only get stronger as you went. I opened the passenger's door, reached in, and grabbed my briefcase from the seat. I turned back to the stone house. David was not in sight. The door was closed. I smiled slightly. The days of him calling the shots were gone for good.

I pushed the front door open and stepped in through the front hall. David was sitting on the couch, where he was earlier, apparently waiting for me. "I'll have that beer now," I told him. He nodded somewhat glumly, as if the whole thing was foretold, and while he was in the kitchen fetching it, I set the briefcase down on a long side table. I reached in and pulled out a signed hard copy of the Professor's memoir and laid it on the table. I scribbled a note on one of the inside pages, as I was often asked to do.

I'd closed the book by the time he returned. He handed me the beer, an Old Style, as I remember. The neck was remarkably cold to my touch. I set it on the table.

"Take a look," I said, pointing to the book, startled for a moment by the gentle look on the Professor's face.

David flipped open the front cover, past a page or two, until he came to the title page and the Professor's signature: "To my dear friend David," it read, and then a space and the signature. He looked up at me, and I motioned for him to turn another page. He did, and on it is my handwriting: "To David, who taught me the ways of the world" and my signature.

He bent over the page, then flipped back to the previous page.

"It's the same handwriting," he said.

At that, I reached around to my back pocket and touched the handle of the kitchen knife. I drew it out slowly. I slipped the blade around and under his neck. I pressed in slightly and pulled until I felt it slip into the flesh. David turned his head toward me. His face was draining. His right arm jerked out.

"The Zippo was the only thing I ever cared about," I said. A weak smirk crossed his face, and his head turned back down. I jerked the knife again, this time more gently, until it gave way into the throat. Blood pumped in huge spurts across the table, strange gurgling, grating sounds rose from beneath my hand, then a blustering noise from my own throat. Everything—the Professor's face, my hands, even the weed still hanging from David's mouth—was a bright crimson. Red liquid far and wide.

I FEEL A cold draft. It means someone has opened the downstairs door. Which means someone is on the stairs. I rise and walk to the door, slide the little bolt, and jerk it open. Nothing, just as before. Still, I feel the cool air. The outside door, I think. Someone is downstairs. I walk to the rear window and look out. No sign of anything, or anyone. I relax.

The stars have settled over the trees. Clouds are shimmering slightly in the reflected moonlight. How many scenes in your life like this have you missed? I think. The unseen beauty of nature. Like today.

It hits me: I am a murderer, after all. Like the Professor, I now know the feeling of taking a human life. Although it didn't happen the way I would have wanted. Clean and clear without emotion or need or hate or guilt was how it should have been. But I had slipped out of neutral. The remnants of the rage reverberate through me, now. Poison left behind, as I said earlier. And that is, I guess, an unfortunate byproduct of clarity. If you wipe the screen clean, you must accept the truth of what then appears. And I will, I'll adjust and move on. There's been so much progress already tonight, and yet more to come. I sense that if—*when*, I mean—the rest of the road is run, adjustments in the emotional content will occur as naturally as the quiet after the storm.

I have no recollection of what happened after the killing; how I got cleaned up—I must have been splattered in blood—or when

I left the place. The knife: I must have taken the time to wash it and put it back in the briefcase. Driving away from the house, out of the city, turning onto the road up here—I don't remember any of it.

Given the track of my life, I must wonder if the story of the killing is true, in whole or in part. For images to spring like that fully formed from nothing and in perfect sequence is quite stunning. To sit here in this room for hours without the slightest hint of the killing scene in the living room of David's house. The recall of it in such exquisite detail should heighten its veracity, I would think. I can't help but smile at the thought that the smirk is finally once and for all wiped from David's face.

But how did it get so out of control? I hadn't gone up there with violent purpose. None at all. I had gone there with some questions, to be sure, some questions about the Aqua Velva Man's violent demise, although I doubt I intended to stir up that nest of devils for the simple reason that David, untrustworthy to begin with, would tell a story that would only make him look good and me weak. If you care about nothing, then you can move through life a free man, unencumbered by mordant emotions, embracing all things, all people; if you quit *trying* to care about something, that is, and yes, I was there, close to there, thanks to my second wife, and I was happier for it. Today was unfortunate from that point of view.

The Zippo.

Long buried deep in the subcutaneous layers, its power never diminished. The motherfucker stole it from me. BANG, the flash of it had hit me, and all plans and intentions shot out the window. It was the singular unmatchable beauty of the chrome case, its built-to-last-forever wheel, the movable steel hinge, the image of it hanging in the long pants pocket of a gyrene stumbling up the sands of some godforsaken island in the Pacific with a rifle clutched in his hand in the face of seething Jap fire. The clink-clunk of it lighting a few Army-issued weeds in the foxhole after purchase on the atoll had been obtained step by bloody step.

There are some critical parts missing, I realize. The rip in my thigh, for example: How did it get there? I pull the torn jean flap back and see the ragged gash, almost completely crusted over now. However it happened, it happened today. I press it hard until pink fluid oozes out around the edges. I close my eyes as the pain shoots into my groin. I suspect the knife slipped from David's neck and sliced into my leg, or maybe he grabbed the hunting knife off the table and slashed back in desperation.

Do I feel bad about the act? you might ask. No, I don't. No guilt or regret. Joy neither, because as I've explained the rage poisoned the beauty of the act. I understand the source of the rage: the Zippo. Now sitting on the table in front of me, right next to the Underwood. Not a drop or smear on it either. A totally unexpected find, incapable of being conjured up by the unstable mind. I tap the silver case once, twice. That, goddamn it, is real.

CLICKETY-CLACK CLICKETY-CLACK clicketyclackclicketyclack. The steady rhythm fills my head and brings me around from my little warren to the scene in the semidarkness of the second-to-last seat in the last car, where the boy and the girl are gathering themselves after their intimate revelations to see what still might lie ahead for them, both sensing as the roaring iron horse gallops down the shivering rails that time is drawing close and yet the stories are not all told. The boy feels it; the girl feels it for him. The girl has admitted to feeling responsible for her brother's death—what could be worse than that?—although she always knew it, has lived with the images of it; whereas the boy, if he is to go forward at all, must plow new ground, or, a better image might be, lean over and peer down into a deep well.

THE GIRL, NOW as clear-eyed and mystical as when she first appeared, leaned forward encouragingly. "There's something else," she said barely above a whisper.

The boy knew the time had come, but he didn't know where to begin. Images crowded against each other. Fragments spun and stopped. Colors blurred and cleared.

FINALLY, THE DOORBELL rang.

"One Saturday morning two detectives came to my house," he began, and the smile faded from the girl's face as she allowed herself to absorb his words. "They claimed they found a wallett in this guy's room. An old queer my friend David knew, who said he would get us a girl if we came to his room. His name was Willie. They showed pictures of him and asked if I knew him. It was David's wallett, and I figured it must have fallen from his pocket when we were . . . when we were in Willie's room."

The last words created images of Willie's place: the soiled curtains puffing in the damp wind, the carved-up dresser with the bottle of aftershave on it, the thin, grubby mattress, Willie's plain brown shoes on the naked wooden floor. The girl shifted slightly in the chair.

"The only reason I went along with it was because Willie promised there would be a girl for us. David said he had met her, seen her naked and played with her tits. Or I wouldn't have gone. I trusted my friend.

The slightest nod back.

"I told the two detectives that I'd never seen the guy in the photo, but they knew better. My mom knew better. I had to lie. They kept holding the wallett up in front of me. 'It's your wallett,' they said. 'It has your name in it. We found it in his room.'"

I told her about the first cop with the river scar on his cheek and the other cop with the small ears. The first cop repeated it. "On the floor," they said. All I could do was shake my head. "It's not mine."

I described Willie, his sharp black eyes and sallow skin, the almost invisible lips, and the sickening smell of the aftershave, as best I could. He told us the girl worked at the state fair and guaranteed she would be over in half an hour. But since he was doing this for us, a favor, he would like a little something back. My friend David was sitting in a chair next to the bed, and he smiled at Willie, and then at me.

"He said he would like to look at us a little. He was staring at me. David nodded. I didn't move, and he nodded again. 'Just pull your pants down,' the man said."

I studied the girl's face for a reaction of disgust, or even curiosity, like a freak show. Myself, so far I felt emboldened by the words. I thought for a moment she was going to reach out and pat my hand, or say something encouraging. I froze, and she must have seen it because she held still.

I AM SLIGHTLY shocked by the growing clarity of the images. They seem more like photos in an album buried in a steamer trunk in the attic of an old house. Black and white, with serrated edges, pasted in a line across stiff black pages. Not quite square. In the next image, the boy is bending over the bed. On the edge of the picture is the arm and bare leg of a man. In the next, the man is holding his dick. The boy's face is sideways on the bed, his eyes closed.

I describe the pictures to the girl. She seems undisturbed.

Going across the black page, the image is of the man settling in on top of the boy, sallow flesh on white. The boy's hand is grasping a chunk of the nubby bedspread; his head has turned the other way, facing the wall, so you can't see his eyes. Eye glasses lay askew in the dull light. One row down, on the edge of the page, the image shows the man on top of the boy, his head tilted back, hands flattened on either side of the boy's head.

The next photo is curled up, and I have to press the corners flat and hold it down by the edges. The boy is half twisted out from under the man, his face wrenched in determination.

Now standing, his jeans up, the boy is holding his glasses in one hand and looking across the room at the door. The photo has a white crease down the middle.

I take one deep breath, then another. My forehead is hot. The girl waits.

The last square is empty; two slots where the corners would be inserted, crusty patches of ancient glue. I press a finger onto the stiff paper, then brush to the right, where the last photo lies flat on the page. The edges are stained brown, but the image in dead center is clear. The boy is bent over the handlebars of his green-and-white Schwinn, his feet pressed back hard on the pedals, water streaming back from the corners of his eyes. On his way to the swimming pool, I told the girl.

THE WINDOW WHIPS open. Bangs against the wall. Autumn has fled; the wind on my face is now warm and moist, a summer wind, like the one blowing on the morning of Joseph's drowning, like the one rousing the curtains in Willie's apartment. The moon settled low over the waters, is growing pale, on its way to one of those see-through discs that hang low in the sky in first light. Now that the screens have been scrubbed free; now that clarity—if not under-standing—has arrived. The wallett had been mine; the detectives that morning had surely insisted on it. I may well have thought oth-erwise at the time, may well have already reconstructed the scene in Willie's room the way I first told it on these pages. It doesn't really matter. Nothing really matters. This scene now, the one I just saw, is as close to reality as necessary. It could have been longer, it could have been shorter, but that's what happened.

I looked in the girl's eyes. She had absorbed the story, me, so deeply into her being—her eyes are open to the depths—that she

cannot separate a response to it, to me. Neither one of us said anything, for there was nothing to say; the story, the images, have disappeared into our shared being.

I RISE AND walk the few steps to the window. The damp wind
has already moistened the leaves, for the close ones glisten in
the paling light. I look down the shore of the lake, to my right,
where the cove is, where the canoe would be if I could see around
the point. Joseph's short life was spent the way it was meant to
be spent. The cold lake water took him down and gave him up.
Nothing could have saved him. Sally survived that day because
her father the caretaker would have killed himself over the loss of
her, too. She's known that for a long time, and she came tonight
to tell me so. Seeing now that even a broken life is sometimes better than none.

The story of Willie and David isn't quite so easy, of course. In
the girl's eyes there is no intimate reaction to it. She sees the scene
as the natural flow of events, as something to be accepted and not
emotionally responded to. My fear of that day fooled me, I see that
now. I must have believed that feelings of shame, and worse, perhaps self-hatred, or immolation, would become who I was. I could
say now that I was wrong, that I would have been able to handle it,
but I couldn't have known that then.

Even now, in the clarity of early morning, I don't hate Willie, I
don't blame him for what became of my life. He was seeking happiness the only way he knew how. Like all of us. As for David, I
should say the same, but I would perhaps wish him some sort of

conscience for what he did, some sort of pain for having betrayed a friendship for whatever it was he was seeking.

Would I have come to this place of clarity, if not understanding, without the girl on the train? I doubt it. Each thread had to be woven into each other just the way it was. The story of her brother, the sad beauty in her exotic eyes. The conductor and the crying baby. Her breasts: I wanted them so badly for my own that I would have done or said almost anything. I remember not long after telling the story of Willie's room that my hands ached for them and only by force of will—and by clutching the Zippo—was I able to hold them still.

The Zippo disrupts this new narrative somewhat. The fact is, after all this time, I am a murderer. I killed David. Out of rage. Thus cheating myself of the joy of the act itself. It makes me question the Professor and his theory of moral neutrality. I don't think the hawk crunches the squirrel's skull in his claws for the fun of it. He does it because nature so decrees it. He does it out of a primal, biological need. To survive. I killed not out of need, or even for pleasure, but to release the rage.

I hold the Zippo up and examine the bottom in the light. "Made in Bradford, PA.," it says in somewhat crude letters. One of a hundred or more that day, probably. I imagine a young woman in the PX in Honolulu holding it steady in her hand while she attaches the Marine Corps emblem on one side, and then turning it over and etching in the initials of a soldier on the other.

So, it would appear in the end of my life that I did care about something. The murder points out the perils of it, you see.

THE GIRL TAPPED the window. "Look," she said. On the far
horizon was a thin band of gray. Dawn was creeping up on the
stars, for the moment still swirling in blue-black.

"Did you see your mother again?" I asked.

Her eyes turned back to me. In them I saw no hesitation, no
challenge. The few hours on the train have given her a look of
acceptance, if not peace.

"Yes," she said softly.

I leaned in a little.

"She came to the funeral. She sat on the far end of the very
last row, by herself. I turned around, and saw her in a black dress.
You could see her eyes through the veil. I looked back after the last
hymn, and she was gone."

She folded her hands. "That was the last time."

I glanced out the window; I could see the engine ahead of us on
a curve. It seemed to be pulling away.

"Did you ever see Willie again?"

"No, never."

The whistle gave two long blasts.

"David?"

I wanted to tell her of this afternoon. But I didn't want her to
see me with blood on my hands.

"He stole the Zippo," I said. "He was the best man at my wedding. He stole it in the robing room after I put on my tuxedo." I
passed on the part of him fucking the bride.

Her eyes lit up a little. "How did you get it back?"

"I took it from him," I said flatly.

Her eyes held questions.

"I took it back."

I looked square at her. She was startled by the violence she sensed, and I saw I was right. I looked away, back out at the plains where in the nocturnal dimness the power lines were slicing the sky into rectangles.

I FEEL THE breeze wash over my face. I close the window and latch it tightly. Time is drawing nigh, as they say. The halo effect around the moon is fading. The top edges of the clouds hovering close by are reflecting a pink sheen. Darkness is my friend. My muse. My collaborator. I feel gratitude for its very existence. Like my winged friend, I doubt I could go forward into the dawning day.

I return to the typewriter with some sense of urgency, to bring the narrative up to date. I turn on the light switch, but it's dead. I type ahead anyway in the waning light of the moon. Did I truly murder David this morning? All of my senses tell me so, and there's the knife lying on the floor. I reach over and pick it up. A smear of blood lingers on the blade close to the sticky handle. I slash the blade through the air and feel a remnant of the rage jerking through my muscles. I see then: the rage is just another feeling, like love or hate or fear, and if you would walk clear and clean into this life you need to be willing to experience it like any other feeling; it has its own charm, its own joy, because of its singular power, and the ability to release it through action, like popping a balloon. You may not seek it out, like you would other emotions—well, we know some do—but when you experience rage you should accept it for its own sake, and the satisfaction that can accompany the sensation of it.

There is no sound coming from the typewriter. My hands are on my lap. I'm finished with the narrative, the one I will leave behind anyway. I pull the last page out and stack it on top of the others, now a good inch or two high. I address it to the Professor's agent and suggest he may want to consider publishing it, as a companion to the other two books. A trilogy. Nonfiction, of course, for cross my heart as I sit here now I believe this to be the best version of events possible, and therefore the truth.

So, there is someone here. I'm pleased to see that. It will be a good feeling to take with me. I would say good-bye to the girl on the train, if I could. I would tell her I've loved her all these years, from the moment she asked me to kiss her. We spoke very little after telling our stories. We drifted off in each other's arms as night fled and a bleak dawn crept across the empty plains. We pulled into the Chicago train yards in a wintry morning light. The locomotives were coal black against a lightly falling snow. A string of brightly painted wooden cars rolled slowly past the window. I spotted the trainman in the caboose at the end and waved like a kid. The girl smiled at this and laid her head on my shoulder.

"No more bandits," she whispered.

Or riders in the sky, I thought.

We understood then that the night would never be over. We would carry it with us for the rest of our days, in our very beings. I stood at the top step of the car and looked into her face and kissed her one last time. Her eyes grew merry, and she whispered something to me, and I saw she hadn't buttoned her coat despite the winter wind blowing outside. One hand and then the other slipped inside and around the soft flesh.

I sat down alone on the second seat from the back, by the window. I watched the girl greet a tall older man dressed in a dark blue suit and overcoat. He leaned down to kiss her on the cheek, then took her bag. The two walked away, toward the station, her arm loosely in his. The last image I have is of her lovely blonde hair lifting in the wind and settling on her gray coat. First love, last love, I think as I stick a final piece of paper in the Underwood and type out the scene.

I RISE AND put on my jacket. I leave the knife where it is. I pick up the Zippo, reach for the door and feel a paper in my inside coat pocket. I hesitate, then pull it out. My name on front; it's the funeral note from my first wife. I open and hold the letter to the moonlight, but cannot read it. I whip the Zippo down across my thigh: Clink! And whip it back up into a blue flame. "Good bye," it says, after my name, "Love," and then her name. I touch the flame to the bottom, watch the paper catch, then hold it until the flame leaps up to my fingers. I have no regrets. The night on the train was a moment of random harmony in my life. That it left me alone for the rest of my days now seems inevitable. I stomp out the sparks in the charred remains.

I flick on the light at the top of the stairs; nothing. Which makes me wonder again about creatures outside or in. The Zippo tosses shadows about on the walls as I descend the stairs to the third floor. I pause at the bottom, but the house is now soundless. Passing my room, I see the chair where I sat by the window the night after Joseph drowned. It pulls me in, but I am determined to keep on moving. In the kitchen, moonlight is pouring in the windows. I flip the Zippo shut. I can see my mother putting sandwiches and apples in paper bags for our lunch at the cove, and then the living room, where my father is sitting in a chair reading the *Saturday Evening Post*. My sister joins me as we leave the front door and step onto the porch, and then she is gone. The darkness outside is lifting. I am feeling good: clear and strong. It was what I wanted, what I predicted if once and for all I could obtain a little clarity.

I pull the door shut behind me. My eye catches a dark blur on the long curve of the road coming in through the pines. A car. Sally is coming to see if I've retrieved whatever she left in the box on the porch. Or perhaps to see me. I feel a shiver of excitement—I can tell her now with ultimate certainty what happened to her brother. Because of the night here, the girl on the train, I know what happened that night in the water. I can tell her of Joseph's panic and convince her that if I had released my life jacket to dive for him we would both have drowned. Final clarity will clear my name in her heart, clear her mind of hate for me. Give her a chance, maybe, at a few decent years left.

The moonlight catches the black top of the sedan. I see a shadow behind the wheel. As the car draws nearer, I can make out the long hair flowing over her shoulders, then her hands on the steering wheel. The car pulls to a stop by the steps leading up to the porch. The driver's door swings open, and a tall female figure steps out. She pauses for a moment, glances up at the house, the high window, then at the box on the corner of the porch. I try to say her name, but I hear nothing. Sally, I try again.

Standing tall and straight, unbending, unyielding, the figure closes the door and walks around the front of the car to the steps.

"Sally," I finally say, and step out from under the eaves, into the moonlight. I raise a hand. She pauses for a moment, seems about to respond, then steps onto the porch.

"Sally," I say again.

She's not ignoring me, I realize, she doesn't hear me. I say her name louder. She hesitates, but it's only a response to the sound of the bats whirling overhead. She steps past me to the corner of the porch, where she bends down and picks up the box. She opens it, examines the contents, and shakes her head in apparent disappointment. She closes the box and glances about her, as if to see whether she's been observed. She walks past me, ethereal, ghostlike in the ease of her movements, so close I could touch her on the shoulder. She reaches for the doorknob, twists it several times, as if to assure herself it's locked. I move to the space between her and the steps.

She pauses for an instant and glances at me. She looks out over the drive and then back to me, not as if she's seeing me, but as if she's feeling me, my presence. Her gaze softens to that of the playful girl on the bank by the river; she is urging me to grab the rope swing and fly far out over the water. Her eyes shine with promise, and I feel the heat of adolescent desire for her. Her eyes stop on my neck; they cloud for an instant before passing on. I touch my neck and feel an odd ridge and something sticky. She shifts the box under one arm, then steps toward me. I force myself to focus and say her name one more time.

"Sally."

She takes a step, and then another. Through me. As if I wasn't there. "It's me," I say. But she is down the steps and moving toward the car. She tosses the box through the open rear window and opens the front door. She scans the window on the fourth floor, as if in a final good-bye, and gets in the car. The door slams noiselessly.

I stand perfectly still until the car has disappeared around the curve and into the pines. I step off the edge of the porch and walk around to the side of the house where I had earlier spotted a vehicle up on blocks. The driver's mirror on the old Ford is intact. I twist it up, to face the moon, and lean over it. I can see nothing because of my shadow. I twist the mirror at a slight angle, until my features slowly appear. I raise my chin a little and lean in closer. There, from one side of my neck to another, runs a thin red ridge. I run my finger over it. The flesh gives, but I feel nothing. I twist my head slightly from side to side; the red line spreads open a little, and I see it crosses both arteries. I raise my finger to my mouth, taste it.

I see it, then, the knife glinting in the mirror over the dresser in David's bedroom. My fingers are touching the edge of the Zippo, and I am figuring out how the lighter ended up there, starting to get pissed, when David's eyes edge onto the mirror. The nervous look is gone, replaced with one I've never seen before. I feel a sting on my neck. A red line zips across the flesh. My head is not wobbling, like Shelley's did, but I can tell from the scarlet flow from one carotid that I must be finished. I manage to grasp the Zippo tightly in my fist. I swing out with it as I turn toward my friend, aiming for his chin. The tension lightens to a smirk as David shifts to his left and my hand glances off his shoulder. He dances back a step, and I begin to fall. My final image is the splash of blood on the colorful weave of the Turkish rug on the polished wood floor.

So, THAT'S THE way it is. I am not the murderer, but the murdered. The clarity of a few moments ago was an illusion. I lean back from the mirror to catch more of my form; it's me, all right, a little worse for wear, eyes a little glassier than usual. Some charge of energy emanating through time and space from the house where I was murdered brought me to this place to unravel the true narrative and lay it out in heaven's light. I tap a knuckle against my front jean pocket. Thunk. I extricate the Zippo from my pocket and grasp it lightly in my fingers. The girl on the train had saved me from oblivion, I see now. I close my eyes to the light; she appears, her mystic eyes slightly somber.

"You know what?" she says. "I remember now that I always wanted to go away to prep school."

Clink. Clunk. I drop the lighter to my side. Glancing a final time at my fourth-story warren, at the curve where Sally's car had disappeared, I walk around the front of the porch, past the steps, until I come to the garden. It is even more wildly overgrown with roses than had been apparent from the window, but somehow less forbidding.

The brick wall is too high for me to climb. I see a hinged wooden door between the wall and the corner of the house. As I pick my way carefully through the thorny vines, a fluttering brushes my ear. A small black form settles on my forearm. The fur tickles as the form folds in its wings.

The gate is rusted shut. I have to kick the latch twice before it swings out. I step through, and from the edge of the cliff I see what appears to be a narrow path winding through the rocks below. The wind has warmed further, and I am grateful for that. I maneuver my way carefully down the side of the cliff, grasping an occasional root to steady myself, until I come to the sharp black rocks at the water's edge. I glance about. The moon, I notice, has disappeared altogether, leaving a faint glow on the far horizon. In a matter of minutes, if not sooner, the edges of the night will begin to fray. The water has calmed; a young boy could get ten skips out of a flat rock on it.

I HESITATE, SUDDENLY alarmed by the unfairness of my imminent demise. I had done nothing wrong. I take a step back from the water's edge. In the moon glow I can see the glint of tiny ripples on the water.

"Now," the girl says, in a tone of gentle encouragement.

She is right; the narrative of my life is now told and set for all time, which is all I've ever wanted, dead or alive. The joy of expiration is as natural as the joy of loving, the joy of killing, the joy of being.

I step in. Icy water fills my shoes. I wait a few seconds and take another step or two.

The water rises over my knees, to my belt. The furry creature has fled my arm and is now resting lightly on my head. I hold the Zippo out in front of me and snap the wheel. Its flame flickers brightly amongst the still-glittery stars. The water is up to my arm pits. I reach back and hurl the Zippo with good force into the night sky; the blue-orange flame tumbles far into the light-speckled blackness and then extinguishes. I hear the whisper of my name in the heavens.

The water fills my nose, rises over my eyes. The creature flutters off into the night. The girl is standing by my side, in front of the Underwood as the scene slowly fades to light.

ACKNOWLEDGMENTS

THE SEED FOR this story was planted one mid-November morning in 2012. Julya (Hulya) and I were a planning a year-long road trip and I was telling my close friend Tom Pace how I was thinking of stopping in small towns along the way and digging up long-ago weird crimes and putting together some sort of true-crime anthology. I can't remember his exact words, but Tom said something like: "You've done true crime. Why don't you try writing with the voice inside your head?" Fiction, he meant; not fiction like a completely made-up story, but fiction that springs from your own, peculiar voice. Two days later, I began knocking out the first page of the manuscript.

Julya and I intentionally provided very little structure for our trip: leaving in July, we would head to New England for early fall and then head down the east coast with stops in Virginia, the Carolinas, and Georgia, ending up in St. Petersburg, Florida, Mexico, and Cuba for the cold months. In the spring we would head to Turkey and Spain. The rest was up for grabs. I had no goal to finish the book on the trip, but the unstructured nature of it, the lack of routine, proved to be the perfect context for the story to evolve.

Wherever we stopped for more than a day, I would work on the manuscript for a few hours. When I had thirty or so pages, I printed it out and asked Julya to read it. We would talk—and often argue—about it over breakfast, while driving, or riding bikes along the shores of Lake Champlain. The book took on a shape of its own, turning this way and that, seemingly of its own accord. Its roots deepened substantially when we spent two weeks at the Vermont cabin of friends, Kathy and Walter Mulica. I wrote every morning for two weeks, and in the grand isolation of their cabin in the mountains, I was able to get a serious glimpse of the road ahead. Finally, months later, at the condo of cousin Bob and Nancy Blue in New Smyrna Beach, Florida, the rest of the story unraveled. I awoke one morning after a week or so and saw the ending. It really was as if the story had been there all along, and the key was releasing it from the burdens of consciousness.

Thus, I am indebted to Tom Pace for the inspiration and the Mulicas and Blues for providing the ideal settings for writing. And thanks to Art Voss, who reminded me of several of my old college Zippo moves, and who pointed out several serious flaws in an early manuscript. Thanks to Scott and friends at the Mayfair Starbucks in Denver, who looked after me during the many hours of writing and rewriting in the place.

Julya's contribution is beyond measure. Her intuitive sense for tone, character development, conversation, and pacing were critical. She slashed excess verbiage with a fine scalpel and rearranged sentences and paragraphs brilliantly. Her patience in the face of my stubbornness was even more remarkable. It made me love her even more.

Agent Paul Bresnick, with his usual skill and commitment, found the right home for the book. I've worked with many editors in my day, but Dan Smetanka, who bought this book for Counterpoint, is far and away the most talented and committed. He had ways of selling proposed changes and new twists to me that made eminent sense. By the end of the editing, I had come to trust his judgment so thoroughly that if there was any doubt on a proposed edit it was resolved his way. In fact, the entire experience with the people at Counterpoint, including publicist Claire Shalinsky and Kelly Winton, has been remarkable. I've been treated there the way an author always hopes to be treated: with respect and courtesy and skilled professionalism.

Present as always, through every step in the creation, was the spirit of my brother, Mike, who so ardently supported my earlier books. How I would love to hear his thoughts on this one.

Printed in the United States
by Baker & Taylor Publisher Services